Welcome to Bitterly Connecticut, hometown of one wistful widow with a very big secret....

She should have been off-limits. After all, Benedetta "Benny" Grady is his best friend's widow. But in the space of a whirlwind week, Daniel Greene went from strong shoulder to lean on to Benny's ardent lover. Now Dan is determined to make Benny his bride. He hasn't waited this long for love to let it get away so easily. But first, Benny has a few ghosts to contend with...

When Benny finds herself pregnant with Dan's child, telling him should be easy. After all, she's fallen hard for the wise-cracking bachelor. But how can she love another while remaining true to her late husband's memory? Could the past hold the key to their future happiness?

Books by Terri-Lynne DeFino

Bitterly Suite
Seeking Carolina
Dreaming August
Waking Savannah

Published by Kensington Publishing Corporation

Dreaming August

A Bitterly Suite Romance

Terri-Lynne DeFino

LYRICAL PRESS
Kensington Publishing Corp.
www.kensingtonbooks.com

For Michael, Karen and Mark, my partners in crime; and for Dotty and Ace, who taught me love.

Acknowledgements

Huge thanks to CoLoNY, my fabulous writing group. Without them, this book would not have happened. An extra thanks to Sharon Struth, who was not only a first reader, but the reason I queried Lyrical Press to begin with.

Thanks also goes out to my Dollbabies, women who not only mean the world to me, but who have supported every effort I have made over the years with enthusiasm and love. A special thanks to Mary who came up with Bitterly Suite.

A humble thank you to my editor, Penny Barber. Her genuine concern for not just the work, but the author, is the stuff of dreams. All writers should be so lucky. Thanks, also, to Renee Rocco, whose efforts to make the road to publication go smoothly are epic. She's pretty funny, too.

As always, the last thanks goes to the one and only Frankie D. I realized long ago that most of the noble heroes in my stories are incarnations of him, these men who see their women struggling to find themselves, and stand back while they do. Waiting. Watching. Completely accepting and loving whoever emerges from the fight, but never interfering with any expectations of his own. It's a rare man who can resist "taming" a woman like me, and instead just hanging on for the ride. That's my Frankie D, and why there is a list of women waiting for me to croak so they can have him.

Chapter 1

When Evening Falls

"You sure you want to do this?"

"Very sure, Harriet. I must."

"That's not exactly true. You could just stay here."

"That's your choice, not mine."

"I never stepped foot outside of this town. Don't 'spect I ever will."

"Then you can?"

"'Course I can. And so can you. You don't have to bedevil that young woman. Just go."

"Bedevil? Harriet, I would never."

"August, you miscreant, you bedevil me constantly."

"Then you should be glad I seek her assistance. You'll be rid of me for all eternity."

"Lot'a'nonsense, far as I'm concerned."

"Only because you are more stuck than you want to believe."

"Stuck? Bah! I'm just waiting."

* * * *

Dirt helped.

Cold earth. Fragrant, moist earth. Under-her-nails, in-the-cracks-of-her-chapped-hands earth. It smelled of snowmelt and leaf mold and worms. Black and rich and crumbly, it was the perfect medium for the colorful pansies planted among the forget-me-nots just starting to pop. Sitting back on her heels, Benny inspected her work.

"What do you think, Henny?" she asked. "Better than impatiens, right? This spot is way too sunny. Maybe we'll do some morning glories this year. I still have that little wooden trellis in the shed. I love morning glories. The blue ones with yellow centers. Yeah, let's do it. I'll stop for seeds on the way ho—"

The nausea banished by dirt swished through her again. She shoved her hands back into the churned-up earth, let the cool fragrance soothe her belly. Swallowing, swallowing, swallowing until it passed. Benny turned to the neighbor. "What do you think, Mrs. Farcus? You like the pansies?"

Again the swell of nausea. Four months. This was supposed to be over. But it hadn't just come in the morning, so why should it stick to the first three months? She'd ask Mrs. Farcus, but she didn't know Benny was pregnant. No one did. And no one would. Yet.

Benny dusted her hands off on the front of her jeans and pushed to her feet. She picked up her trowel and the empty bag from the soil, bent again to grab the plastic potting containers and nearly vomited right there in the garden she'd just spent the last hour planting. Leaning heavily upon the tombstone, she screwed her eyes tight until it passed.

"Hey, Benny? You okay?"

Her eyes flew open and she was grateful for the dark fringe of hair obscuring her face. It gave her a moment to hide all she did not want anyone else to see. Straightening, she waved to Charlie McCallan standing with one foot in and one foot out of his truck. "I'm fine, Charlie. No worries. Just hungry. I think I forgot to have lunch."

Instead of waving back and moving on, he closed the door and started up the rise toward her. Benny choked down the panic. Could he see? Did he know? But Charlie was squinting into the sunlight, smiling the same smile she'd known since they were young and she was his best pal's pesky kid sister. Benny tried to relax.

"It gets more extravagant by the year," Charlie said. He brushed dirt from the grey stone. "I see you did up Mrs. Farcus's plot too. As always."

"She's an old friend."

"She died nearly a century before you were born, Benny." Charlie laughed softly. "She's my great-whatever grandmother."

Benny looked up. "Really? How did I not know that?"

"Didn't know my family went back so far? Why would you?"

"Because I haunted this cemetery as a kid."

Charlie's eyebrow quirked, but he said nothing of her horrible pun. "Harriet was one of three daughters," he said instead, "so the name Gardner died out here in Bitterly, but I have Farcus cousins somewhere."

"I wonder why she's buried alone."

"Her husband, I think his name was Josiah, died out west somewhere about six months before she ever found out. That's the story, anyway."

"So sad."

"It's nice of you to pretty-up her grave too."

Benny shrugged. "I always bring too many flowers."

"You okay?"

Her gaze moved to the tombstone easier to look at than Charlie's familiar concern.

Henderson Parker Fredericks
June 3, 1976 ~ August 20, 2010
Beloved Husband

Benny-and-Henny, a joint moniker earned in high school that carried through to the day he crashed his motorcycle barely a mile from their home. Now she was Benny-without-Henny, and the hole he left in her gaped just as wide and as deep as it had six years ago.

"I'm okay, Charlie. Really."

"Why not come to the bakery with me? Johanna's still got some shepherds-pie-pies left from lunch. You'd be doing us a favor if you take some. They're not as good the next day. The crust gets soggy."

"I'm sure you and your ridiculously large family will find use for them."

"Do you know how often we eat shepherds-pie-pies?"

They laughed together. Benny's belly churned. "I'll have to pass. You know my mother. She's already made dinner enough to feed the whole town. But thank you. And say hi to Johanna for me."

"Will do." He started back to his truck. "And say hey to your brother for me. Tell him to come home once in a while. I haven't seen him since the reunion."

"He is home," Benny called. "In North Carolina."

"Bitterly is home. Always. Whether he likes it or not."

Benny shook her head, waved him off and finished tucking her tools into the daisy-dotted canvas carrier she bought two years ago and subsequently had inked into the tattoo covering most of her right arm. Her trowel. The forget-me-nots. The always-reliable marigolds and snapdragons. Last year's impatiens. This year she would add the pansies, thus marking her gardening calendar as only Benedetta Marie Grady would, no matter what her mother thought of tattoos.

She pushed back her sleeve, peeking at the first tat inked, on the first anniversary of Henny's death—a little blue forget-me-not, there on the underside of her wrist. In the six years since her husband's death, Benny added steadily to her sleeve. A tribute to Henny, and the garden she kept for him, there on her arm.

"Forever, baby," she told the tombstone. "I promised you forever, and I meant it."

Her hand moved to her still-mostly-flat belly that had never actually been flat in her whole life, but she stopped herself, closed her eyes to the impulse until it passed. A promise was a promise, and Benny knew straight down to her superstitious-Italian soul that breaking this one was even less of an option than stepping on a crack in the sidewalk, or refusing to wish on birthday candles.

"Ah, Henny." She squatted on her haunches again, pinching off a spent flower she hadn't earlier noticed. "You make it very hard to leave Bitterly, but I have to. If I stay, everyone will know, and…well…anyway. I won't be gone long, and it'll be winter, so it won't matter so much, right? I'll come back after I figure things out. I just want to do it without everyone hovering. You know how my family is. And then there's Dan—"

Benny spun to the tap on her shoulder and thumped flat onto her bottom. No Charlie or anyone else who might have snuck up on her while she confided in her dead husband. Benny found only herself among the tombstones. She looked narrowly in Mrs. Farcus' direction.

"Are you playing games with me, you old trickster?"

No answer. Of course. Mrs. Farcus never answered, not once in all the years Benny had been talking to her grave. Neither did Henny, for that matter.

Benny laughed, a sound as hollow as it felt. She picked herself up, brushed herself off, and hurried to her motor scooter before either of her ghosts decided to finally oblige.

* * * *

Benny twirled her spaghetti with no intention of eating it. Tomato sauce gave her the worst heartburn in the history of heartburn. When she thought no one was looking, she shoved a forkful into her mouth as she rose from the table and headed straight for the garbage can in the corner of the yellow kitchen.

"Don't even think about it, young lady." Clarice Irene Grady descended upon her daughter with all the intensity of an Italian mama intent upon feeding her young. She yanked the full bowl of spaghetti and meatballs from Benny's hand. "You hardly touched it."

"I'm not hungry. I…I went to CC's on the way home from the cemetery. Charlie said there were a whole bunch of pie-pies left over. You know how I love them. I'm sorry, Ma. I couldn't resist."

"Ah, you should have brought one home for me." Peadar Grady gazed heavenward, his hands patting his paunch. "There's no bit of heaven like one of Johanna Coco's pie-pies. You make me jealous, girl."

"I'm sorry, Daddy." Benny kissed his forehead. "Next time. I promise."

"What am I to do with all of this?" Clarice held up the plate. "I cook a good meal and you stop on the way home for—"

"Give it here, Ma." Benny's brother Peter held out his hand. "I'm ravenous."

"And if you don't stop eating like a horse you'll be as big as your father."

"Then throw it away. See if I care."

Clarice plonked the plate on the table in front of him, glared at Benny and huffed to the stove, muttering. Benny mouthed, *thank you* to Peter. He winked and tucked into her uneaten meal. Tall and lean and muscular, her baby brother didn't have an extra ounce on his body and never had. Neither had their father in his younger years, as Clarice was fond of reminding him. Still she fed him as if he'd been starved half his life, and would continue starving for the rest of it if not for her efforts.

Benny headed into the parlor, as her mother preferred to call it, and to the interior stairs leading up to the second-story of the two-family house. Seven years, she and Henny had lived there. Six years alone. She wasn't sure if the notion that she would never leave her familial home comforted or smothered.

"It's movie night," Clarice called after her. "You coming back down?"

"Sure, Ma."

If having her way were actually an option, Benny would take a long bath, curl into bed, and be asleep before dusk gave way to dark. But—

All ways here, you see, are the Queen's ways.

The urge to push against every one of Clarice's shoves had once been automatic. It diminished year by year. It wasn't only because her mom had been her rock after Henny's death, Benny just didn't have it in her anymore. After a shower, Benny would be downstairs again, plopped on the couch she'd been plopping into all her life, to watch a romantic comedy starring one of the British Dames her mother was mad for.

In the privacy of her own apartment, Benny smoothed her hands over her belly. She imagined it rounding, swelling, exploding, and her mother's extraordinary, if slightly embarrassed, joy after it had.

Clarice had been dreaming of grandchildren since her own brood turned from childhood to adolescence. Grandchildren provided within a year of a wedding and at a rate of every other year thereafter. But Tim married and moved to North Carolina before the first was born. Peter hadn't even had a serious girlfriend yet. And in the seven years of Benny's marriage, there had not even been a suspected *oops*. She and Henny wanted to see the world first. They planned to backpack across Europe, to book passage on a cargo vessel sailing from California to Japan, to work the vines in Napa a full season. Seven years of planning adventures they never took.

Then he died.

No Henny. No adventures. No baby.

Until now.

Benny moved like a ghost through her apartment, closed all the windows. The beautiful day was becoming a chilly dusk. Nights were usually cold in Bitterly, even when summer days spiked in the nineties. The trees, the river, the sheltering Berkshire Mountains absorbed the heat, stored it away for the long winter. A winter she would miss. Along with the autumn splash in the mountains. She would be in North Carolina with her brother, Tim, and his family. Where it was hot. Even at Thanksgiving and Christmas. And she would have a newborn Clarice didn't even know about. A baby born in sorrow, whose daddy was not Henny.

Benny couldn't breathe. She needed out. Now. She bolted to the door, yanked it open, and pounded down the exterior stairs leading to the yard. She jammed the helmet on her head, kicked her scooter to life, and sped off before her mother could shout her name, even if Benedetta saw her at the back screen door.

* * * *

The bakery was still open. During the summer months, CC's North often hopped long after the posted six o'clock closing. It was only June and unseasonably cool, but it was still light enough to pass for daytime. The doors of the bakery were open wide.

Benny slipped off her scooter. Adjusting her getting-tight jeans, she followed the scent of baking into CC's and stopped dead in her tracks.

"Oh." She forced her feet to walk her into the bakery. "Hey."

"Hey, yourself."

"How are…what have…Valentine's getting so big."

"Yeah, I hear kids do that."

Benny quelled the urge to press her palms to burning cheeks already giving away too much. Dan Greene shifted the toddler in his arms. Waiting? What could he be waiting for? Benny pretended she didn't know exactly what and instead moved to the counter, her back to him.

"Jo!" he called, startling both her and the baby. "Come get your kid. I have to go home."

Johanna Coco McCallan pushed through the swinging door, arms outstretched. Flour on her cheek, long hair in a knot on top of her head, she swooped past Benny with a look of surprise and a wave before scooping her daughter from Dan's arms.

"Sorry, Dan. I didn't realize—"

"No worries." He kissed the baby's round cheek. "Will I see you and Charlie for my niece's graduation party?"

"We'll be there. Caleb will be watching the bakery, but we'll have Tony and Millie with us."

"I'll let my sister know. See you, Jo. Benedetta."

Benny waved over her shoulder, eyes resolutely on the menu board.

"Curiouser and curiouser."

Johanna's voice turned Benny around. There were others in the bakery. They sat at tables, sipping coffee out of to-go cups from the coffeehouse next door. It was a deal Johanna struck when first she opened her bakery in Bitterly—she wouldn't serve coffee if the coffeehouse didn't serve baked goods. The result was a sort of co-op suiting not only the two businesses, but the town as well.

"What's curiouser?" Benny held out her arms for Valentine, a chubby little cherub as fixed an icon in CC's as Johanna's mud cookies and shepherds-pie-pies.

Johanna handed her over. "Dan. I usually have to pry Valentine from his arms before he'll give her up."

"She's a special girl." Benny's heart pounded. "I don't blame him."

"Well he was sure in a hurry to hand her off just now." Johanna pulled the elastic from her hair, piled it high again and secured it in place. "Did someone say something to him?"

"I only just walked in." She bounced the baby, avoiding Johanna's eyes. "Dad was hoping for some of your pie-pies. Any left?"

"One or two. Charlie said you turned him down."

"I did. Out at the cemetery. When I got home, Dad was inconsolable that I would pass up a pie-pie."

"Then I'll go grab one for him. You mind holding her?"

Benny clutched Valentine closer. "Try taking her."

Johanna scooted around the counter and into the back. Valentine watched her mother vanish, but didn't cry. Smiling a wet, baby smile, she reached for Benny's turquoise pendant.

"No you don't." She tapped it away from the baby's mouth, but not out of her hand. Valentine studied the blue stone, her baby brow furrowed with thoughts Benny couldn't begin to guess at. Would she dream in blue that night? Holding the baby closer, Benny closed her eyes and allowed her own tremulous joy rumble through her.

A boy. She was positive. And already, she loved him so much.

"Here you go," Johanna came at her, the bagged pie-pies outstretched and already spreading buttery patches in the paper sack. "Tell him he got the last two."

"I'll trade you." She offered Valentine, who reached for her mother with a little squeal. Benny grabbed the sac. "Crap. I didn't bring any money."

"I'm not charging you for leftovers, Ben."

"They're not leftovers until tomorrow."

"They're leftovers the minute lunch is over. Seriously, don't be weird."

"Thanks, Jo."

Johanna waved away her thanks. "Now if I can get these laggers out of here, I can go home. I should have gotten Dan to do it before he left. He's good at clearing a room."

Benny laughed along with Johanna, even if it made her woozy. Funny man, Dan Greene. Always joking, lightening even the darkest moments. Dependable. Loyal. Kind. Everyone's favorite plow man in winter, landscaper the rest of the year even if he liked to pretend he was an ornery old bachelor and dedicated grouch. It was part of his charm, and Benny had always liked that about him until she more than liked him for it, which was entirely unacceptable.

"How are you doing, Ben?"

Benny bit her lip. "I'm okay. Just—you know. Same old, same old. I—I hear Nina is coming back to the States for the holidays."

"You heard right. And she's bringing back a surprise."

"Nina? A surprise? That doesn't sound like her."

"I know, right?" Johanna laughed. "But she's not talking. I'm dying of curiosity."

While those stragglers finished up and left, while Johanna tidied up the front and her stepson did the same in back, Benny listened to her talk and talk and talk. About Nina and the trendy but authentic Curiosity Shop she and Gunner founded in New York City. About the honeymoon Johanna and Charlie finally took, meeting her sister and brother-in-law in Bora Bora, sailing those South Seas islands that never stopped being exotic. As long as Johanna kept talking, Benny didn't have to say a word. Any wondering about Daniel Greene was safely off topic, even if the conjured image of him so tenderly holding Valentine would not quit. And then there was the way he looked at her the moment she first walked in.

She rode her scooter home in the dark, the only light coming from the stars overhead.

Star light, star bright,

First star I see tonight.
I wish I may, I wish I might,
Have this wish I wish tonight.

Benedetta revved the tinny engine, pretended the tears instantly drying on her cheeks came from forgetting her goggles in her rush to be out of the house. They had nothing to do with Dan, or the gentle way he held Valentine, or how her heart had stuttered that moment before she forced it to still.

* * * *

"Don't come through the kitchen. I just washed the floor."

Dan Greene grumbled under his breath, pulled his work boots off and tiptoed across the kitchen floor already dry anyway, to the mudroom opening into the breezeway and separating the kitchen from the family room. He made a show of closing the door loudly.

"Thank you," his sister called as she came through the kitchen carrying a load of laundry.

"Hey! You told me to stay off the floor."

"My feet are clean."

"So are my socks."

"I was afraid you'd walk on it with your boots." Evelyn offered him her cheek, which Dan dutifully kissed. His sister looked tired, more so than usual. He took the laundry basket from her and loaded clothes into the washer.

"I can do it," she said.

"You can't do it while fixing me a plate of whatever's left from your little scavengers' dinner."

Evelyn pursed her lips. "I thought you were bringing home pie-pies."

Dan shoved the last of the laundry in, closed the door a smidge too forcefully. Benedetta had walked into the bakery and all thought walked out of his head. If he wasn't sure before, her behavior in the bakery cinched it—Benny wasn't just avoiding him, she was trying to pretend he didn't exist.

"I forgot," he said. "I was playing with Valentine."

"She's a sweet little thing. How is Johanna?"

"Fine. Why wouldn't she be?"

"No reason. Just making conversation. Come and sit. I'll fix you a plate."

Dan did as he was told, as he always did what his older sister asked of him. And even what she didn't. Like putting the laundry in when she was so tired the weariness manifested in deep splotches under her eyes. Like selling the cramped but adequate house they'd bought together after their parents died, to move into hers when Paul left her sick and struggling. Sitting at the table, he tucked into the warmed egg noodles and peas while Evelyn took cold fried chicken from the fridge.

"Not a fit supper for a man who works as hard as you," she said.

"Better'n what I'd have made for myself, back in the day."

"Back in the day"—she snorted—"you were young and could eat mothballs on toast and then go out frogging all night long."

"You saying I'm old?"

"I'm saying you're older. We both are." Evelyn sat opposite him. A bulb was out in the overhead fixture, casting even deeper shadows under her eyes. Dan worried about her, about keeping up with the kids, her job, and the constant battle with Lyme disease left untreated for too long. "Eat," she said. "It'll be disgusting if I heat it up again."

"How are the plans for Mabel's graduation party going?" he asked around a forkful of peas. "Oh, yeah, Jo, Charlie and the younger kids will be here."

"No Caleb?"

"Someone's got to mind the store."

Evelyn grinned. "Mabel's going to be disappointed. She has a little crush on him."

"He's too old for her."

"He's only seventeen, Dan. She's off to high school next year."

"There's a big difference in them three years right now."

"I suppose." Evelyn sighed. "Plans are going fine."

"Something wrong?"

"Just tired."

"Did you make an appointment with your doc yet?"

"I will."

"When?"

"Tomorrow."

"You've been saying all week. Come on, Ev. You think I want to raise your brats if you croak?"

She laughed. "They do have a father."

Who they hadn't seen since Christmas. "Paul'd take them out to Denver. You don't want your kids raised with all the weirdos out there."

"You're awful, Daniel."

"Just make an appointment. Putting it off is what got you in the first place."

"I know. You're right." She pressed palms to the table and pushed herself to her feet. "I'll call right now and leave a message. Okay?"

"Heat me some more noodles while you're up." He held out his plate. "Please?"

Evelyn swatted him in the back of the head, but she took his plate and spooned more noodles onto it. Sticking it into the microwave, she talked to her doctor. Dan listened carefully to the message she left —a vague name, number, and, please-call-back-at-your-earliest-convenience.

"There. Happy now?" His sister put his plate in front of him, set the phone on the table.

"You going to follow up tomorrow?"

"If they don't call? Of course."

He frowned. She was more stubborn than he was, and the reason why something a course of antibiotics could have fixed became a lifelong disease she would never quite escape. Dan knew she wouldn't call the doc back any more than the doctor's office would return her call.

A bump upstairs lifted both their heads. Evelyn rolled her eyes. "Joss must be trying to fly again. I'd better go see. You okay eating by yourself?"

"I ate by myself a long time, Ev. Go."

A squeeze to his shoulder, and his sister left him. Dan listened to her tread up the stairs, to her voice if not the words she said to her son. Picking up the phone, he hit the redial button.

"This is Daniel Greene," he said. "Evelyn Taylor's brother. She just left you a message to give her a call back. Now I'm leaving you a message to make sure you do."

Chapter 2

Spirits of the Winds and Leaves

"It's going to rain. Let me drive you."

"Ma, come on." Benny adjusted her goggles. "I'm thirty-six years old. When are you going to stop treating me like a baby?"

"I worry about you on this thing."

"It's a scooter. It doesn't go over thirty miles per hour."

"People have been killed at lesser speeds."

"Where do you get your facts from?" Benny glanced skyward. The cloud-cover was definitely thickening, getting darker. She leaned forward and kissed her mother's cheek, revved the hair-dryer-like engine. "I'm going to see Henny after work, so don't wait dinner for me."

"I'll leave it in the oven."

Benny pulled away. Clarice's voice, whatever she was saying, faded. Her mother would watch her until the road curved and took her precious baby from sight, wring her hands, and then head back up the driveway, shaking her head as she went. Benny didn't have to see the scene to know it by heart.

"How do you stand it?" she'd asked her brother once. Peter had smiled and shrugged.

"She's Ma. She can't help it. I don't mind having someone cook all my meals and wash my laundry."

"Because you're still in your twenties and unattached," Benny said. "Wait until you have a serious girlfriend. Or a wife. There is a reason Tim lives in North Carolina."

Another smile, a sadder one. Another shrug, half-hearted. While she and Tim were a respectable four years apart, Peter was a full decade younger than Benny. The *oops*-baby born long after her parents thought it could happen. He'd been everyone's baby, the favorite of every teacher he ever had. At twenty-six, despite the personality and appearance that had the ladies beating down the doors, he remained a devout and determined mama's boy.

The first raindrops fell. Benny twisted the throttle, pushing the scooter to its limits. The scooter sailed into the gravel lot just as the skies released. She did not like being late, even if there were such a thing at Savvy's. The place opened when it opened, closed when it closed, and as long as the employees got their work done, her boss was happy.

"For goodness sake, Benny. I'd have come to get you. Why didn't you call?"

"It's fine, Savvy. I got here before the rain."

"Barely." Savannah—Savvy—Callowell looked her up and down. "You sick?"

Benny gulped. "No. Do I look that bad?"

"Now don't be defensive. You just look a little…stressed, I suppose."

"You live with my mother and then talk to me about stress."

Savannah laughed, the might of her single quirked eyebrow easing. Benny had been one of the first applicants after this small black woman bought the old Larson farm in very white Bitterly, Connecticut six years ago. After the stir died down, Larson's quickly became Savvy's to all but the oldest residents, and Savannah became a good friend.

"So, what's up for today? You want me to get started on the tomatoes?"

"Let's go to my office." Savannah turned away without waiting for a response.

"What is it?" Benny hurried after her. "What's wrong? Did I leave the hose on again? Your office flooded, didn't it?"

"No, Benny." She gestured Benny in, flicked on the lights and crossed to her desk. Twisting in her red-leather-rolly-chair, Savannah clicked at her keyboard. "Do you have something you want to tell me?"

"Tell you?" Sweat beaded Benny's upper lip. She forced her hand to keep away from her belly. "About what?"

"All those late nights. I wondered what you were doing."

"I wasn't doing…I mean, I was, but…" One week of being the nearest thing to happy she'd been in six years. One week! "How did you know? I thought no one—"

"Well, sugar, why did you let it go live if you didn't want me to know about it?" She pushed away from the computer, motioned Benny in. "It turned out really beautiful. Thank you, Benedetta. I forgot all about that picture you snapped of me."

Savannah smiled back at her from the screen, short hair coiled into spikes and dirt on the white tank top accentuating every farm-chiseled muscle in her thin arms. The blur over her left shoulder Benny had cropped out at least a half-dozen times was still there, but otherwise, it looked damn good.

"I totally forgot about this," Benny said. "It's just a blogger site. I scheduled it to go live and then—" She spread her fingers. "I've been a bit preoccupied lately. Sorry, Savvy. I meant to tell you so you could tweak it if you wanted."

"I don't know the first thing about blogging."

"It's simple, and fun. You can write daily posts or weekly or whatever you want, but all the information anyone needs to find your farm and what it's about is right there on the main page. There are links to pictures and a few testimonials I might have made up but are completely true. Do you like it?"

"I love it." Savannah took both Benny's hands and gave them a squeeze. "You're a wonder."

"I was bored and couldn't sleep. I'll give you the sign-in and password. It's all yours."

"Will you show me how to…tweak it? Is that the right word?"

Benny laughed, this time without the queasy feeling. "Sure. I'll pull up another chair."

* * * *

Despite Savannah's assertion she knew nothing of computers or social media, she caught on quickly. By lunchtime, Benny was out in the greenhouse, nibbling at a sandwich and thinning blossoms off the tomatoes finally ready to be planted in the ground now that all danger of frost was done.

"Too many on one stem doesn't give them enough room to grow," Savannah once told her. Benny hated denying even one blossom its chance at becoming a tomato, but she'd been working at Savvy's long enough to know her boss was right. It still bothered her every time.

She forced herself to eat her lunch. All the prego-books she read said she'd start showing soon. Tall as she was, she'd never been supermodel thin. Voluptuous, Henny used to call her. She preferred the exotic sound of *zaftig*. Keeping her curves would buy her another month, maybe two before her pregnancy became too obvious. If her mother found out, it was all over. Worse would be for Dan to figure out that Valentine's Day had gotten him a bit more than laid.

She had to tell him. She had to. What kind of woman, what kind of mother kept a good man from his child?

Benny plucked, ate. Not only did Dan have the right to know his child, their child had the right to know his father. Not even her most confused and reluctant moment chased that knowledge from Benny's head. But how? When? What would she say?

Hey, Dan. Remember the night we had sex in the carriage, in the cold, under the stars? You do know how babies are made, right? Well, we made one. Henny's wife and his best friend, bumping uglies in public. So much for loyalty, eh?

Even as a joke, the thought made her nauseous, so nauseous she couldn't finish her sandwich. The same had been happening since the lines first appeared on the pee-stick. Soon, she kept telling herself. She would tell him soon. But soon never came, because the nausea always hit, because the guilt of producing life when Henny was dead simply turned her brain to mush.

"Good Lord, sugar, if you don't look like you're about to go down." Savannah's arm went around her waist, supporting her when she didn't even realize her knees were starting to buckle. She helped Benny to an overturned crate, sat her down, pressed a cool hand to her forehead. Benny closed her eyes. She willed the nausea and the thoughts to subside. A moment, two, and she started to feel better.

"I won't ask what's going on," Savannah said. "You won't tell me if I do, but please see a doctor about whatever this is ailing you."

"I know what's wrong with me," Benny started, but pulled herself up short. "Too many late nights drinking and partying with my friends."

"Very funny."

"Would you believe I'm an avid gamer who stays up playing online with people I've never met in the flesh?"

"I would, but no, that's not it either." Savannah cocked her head. She pursed her lips. She looked about to say something, but turned away instead. The hand moving to and dropping quickly from her brow was as slight as the way the corners of her eyes suddenly pinched, but Benny noticed.

"Valerie got here a few minutes ago," Savannah said. "She can finish this. You rest a bit, Benny, and then go home. Dr. Callowell's orders, y'hear?"

"Yes, ma'am," Benny tried to tease, but Savannah had already turned away. Her steps were hurried, as if she were fleeing something but didn't want that something to know. It wasn't the first time Benny noticed this, or the ephemeral sensation of spider-webs on skin that accompanied it. Still, she let it slide. At the moment, she had her own sensations to deal with.

Benny forced the remainder of her lunch down, rested a few moments in the cool office and went home. Only she didn't go home.

Riding the still-wet roads to the cemetery, Benny breathed in the cool, washed-clean air. It settled the queasiness she was convinced came as much from anxiety as it did her pregnancy. She anticipated the muddy earth awaiting the morning glory seeds in her pocket, the flowers needing dead-heading, and filling the bare spot on Mrs. Farcus' plot with the marigolds riding in the milk crate bungee-corded to the back of her scooter.

Turning her scooter into Bitterly Cemetery, the familiar peace descended. As a devoted teenaged-goth-chick, Benny had done the black eye-liner and lipstick, wore ironic t-shirts and hung out at the cemetery with all the other goth kids. Whatever trendy, put-on reason her friends might have had, the cemetery wasn't a place of dead bodies and séances to brave on Halloween Night for Benny. It was a place of peace, of rest.

She used to stroll among the stones, looking at the dates and wondering about the lives lived between them. She made up stories, and sometimes found histories in the library. Harriet Gardner Farcus had been one of those histories. The daughter of one of the founding families, she'd married the son of another. She was born, lived and died in Bitterly, never having stepped foot outside its confines. It hadn't been difficult to find stories about her. Midwife and herbalist, Harriet Farcus had also been known to foster any orphaned animal left upon her doorstep. Benny liked to think of her as a benevolent witch in a land that no longer believed in such things. When Henny died and Benny realized a plot near her was vacant, she had wept tears of joy.

Leaving her scooter in its usual spot under the shade tree, Benny went first to Henny's grave. The garden was a bit soggy, but nothing squashed. She dead-headed spent flowers and planted the morning glories, blew her husband a kiss and turned to Harriet's grave.

"What the—?" She spun, and spun again. That tap. Another one. Benny gritted her teeth. Squinting, she scanned the area for someone who might be tossing sticks or little stones. There was no one, and neither were there any bits of stick or stone on the meticulously cared-for grass.

Benny inhaled deeply, glanced at her husband's grave, and took her marigolds to Mrs. Farcus.

"I don't know what the heck is going on here, Mrs. Farcus," she murmured as she dug the hole. "I'm not imagining it. Yesterday, I could convince myself. But again today? Am I hallu—"

Again the tap, this time, harder. Benny spun to her right to find no one there, only empty air that felt strangely emptier than the air to her left. No stone in the grass. No bird or bee or anything but the silent cemetery and late afternoon sunshine. She glanced at Harriet's marker.

"Is it…is it you? Are you…?" Benny shook her head, chuckled softly. "Don't be stupid, Benedetta. You're addled these days, is all."

Her hand moved to her belly. Aside from the tech at the childbirth clinic, no one knew. Necessary as it was, it felt like betrayal, like she was unhappy, like she didn't want the baby she kept secret. Her hand still on her belly, she touched Harriet's marker.

"I'm pregnant." The words rushed out in a breath exhaled. "I'm going to have a little baby in November. I think it's doing strange things to me. I keep feeling—" A sound like wind, and again the tap. Concentrated. Harder. Benny startled, but she didn't turn. "Who…who are you?"

This time, not a tap, but a gentle squeeze that lingered like comfort. Benny closed her eyes. "If it's you, Harriet, give me a squeeze."

Nothing. Tears welled. Could it be…?

"Henny? Is it you? Oh, please. Please let it be you."

No squeeze, just the lingering sensation of a hand on her shoulder. Benny squeezed her eyes tight. The tears welling fell free. Not Harriet. Not Henny. Definitely someone, or something, trying to get her attention. Or she was completely losing it, once and for all. Opening her eyes again, she didn't turn to look, but peeked out of the corner of her eye. Nothing stirred the air beside her. Still the silent cemetery, still sunshine, but the touch did not fade.

"Please. Who are you?"

The spectral hand lifted, but did not fall away. She felt fingers in her hair, a breath upon her neck, and single word whispered into her ear.

August.

Chapter 3

See Not As the Eyes of Man

"Here she comes, Harriet. Here she comes."

"Calm yourself. I see her."

"What do I say?"

"What are you asking me for? She's been talking to me since she was a child and I never felt the need to answer. This is your idea, August, not mine. You're the one who wants out of here so bad. Figure it out."

"You're just angry because I'm leaving you."

"Angry for the first peace and quiet in donkey's years? Not likely."

"You'll be lonely, when I'm gone."

"You think you're such good company? Go on. Off with you, before I box your ears."

"If you haven't noticed, I don't have ears."

"I'll box them anyway. Don't test me 'less you want to find out."

* * * *

Benny stayed away from the cemetery for a few days. It wasn't hard. Between tending the newly planted fields and selling flowers to the locals sprucing-up their gardens, June was a very busy time at the farm. The blog brought even more customers to Savvy's. New Yorkers 'in the country' for the summer came in their never-seen-a-dirt-road SUVs and filled them with flats of annuals. Benny liked watching the kids' faces when they saw the baby animals. They never made the connection between those in the pen and the grain-fed, cruelty-free meat Savannah sold discreetly out of a walk-in around back. She stocked not only beef and pork and chicken, but venison, goose, turkey and, occasionally, bear supplied by local hunters. The goat cheese and soaps sold in-store were made by an old high school friend of Benny's, Darla, and her wife, Sandra. They traded their services for all the wool they could shear, card, spin, dye, and knit into the textiles they sold out of their shop in town. Benny already had her eye on one of their baby blankets.

Three days of guilty avoidance passed before she caved and headed for the cemetery. How would she stay away for months?

Riding through the dusk, she flew between the gates minutes before the cemetery officially closed, even though there was really no such thing for Bitterly Cemetery. In the earliest days of her widowhood, when summer still made nights cool instead of cold, Benny pitched the tent she and Henny bought for the big camping trip they never took, and slept at his graveside, waiting. If she believed hard enough, he'd find a way to her. And Benny believed. She felt whole worlds just beyond her fingertips when she stretched her arms out wide. It was there. She simply could not reach it. Yet.

August.

The word bounced about Benny's head, clear as it did three days ago. August was the month Henny died. Was it connected in any way? Or did it mean whatever it was trying to reach her would do so in August? Tossing and turning through the night, Benny tried to make herself believe it was, after all, Henny trying to contact her, and that on the anniversary of his death, something would happen. But there had been no squeeze when she asked. In her heart, she knew it wasn't him. She never felt Henny in the cemetery, despite her almost-daily visits, only an empty space he used to fill up.

Flopped on the ground beside his tombstone, arms behind her head, gazing at the clouds, Benny let go a long sigh. "Sorry I haven't been here. I got totally freaked out the other day." She rolled onto her side. Flowers needed dead-heading. She plucked at a few. "That's not quite right. I didn't get freaked out. I got hopeful. But it's not you trying to get my attention. You have it already, don't you, Henny. All of it. Almost. This is just so weird. All the years I did séances with my friends and dabbled in Wicca even though it made Ma's head explode, I wished so hard to see something otherworldly, and now this…whatever it is. Part of me says it's bullshit. Part of me says *finally!* But I want it to be you, Henny. I just want it to be you."

Habit rolled Benny onto her belly and she instantly felt the pressure across her swelling abdomen. Burying her face into her folded arms, she inhaled the earthy scent. In. Out. The grass, newly cut. The dirt still damp from its daily watering. Intoxicating in its way. And the pressure across her abdomen a real and unavoidable reminder of the child she carried. Not Henny's. Dan's. A man she had known all her life, yet barely knew at all.

"I was lonely," she told the grass and earth. "And he is…he's Dan. He did that stupid, does-this-smell-funny thing one day at CC's and I fell for it. He wiped the cream from my nose so tenderly, you know? And when he said I needed to get out of the house, and who better than a harmless old bachelor friend, I said yes before I even thought about it." Another deep breath in, out. "I didn't realize how much I missed laughing. We had fun. When he asked if I wanted to go to the movies, I said yes. Another dinner? Yes. He showed up at the house with that horse and carriage of his on Valentine's Day and took me for a ride. That was the night, Henny. It was the only time we—well, you know how babies are made."

She sniffed back tears.

"He told me he was falling in love with me. Why did he have to say those words and ruin it all? I've been avoiding him all these months, knowing I couldn't forever. Knowing it was wrong. This is his baby too, right? When I saw him at CC's the other day, I didn't know how to act, what to say. I—I think I miss him. There. I said it out loud. I miss Dan. I miss the way he made me laugh and how he made me feel. And now you know. But you have all along, haven't you? You saw me with him, didn't you?"

Tears spilled into sobbing. She had put it out of her mind, the notion Henny had watched his wife, the woman who promised him forever, make love to another man. It didn't matter it was Dan. Good guy Dan. Funny guy Dan. Old high school buddy Daniel-freaking-Greene. It would have been better if he'd been a stranger, or some asshole she wouldn't think a second thought about. Sex was biology. Making love was an entirely different thing.

A touch, first cold, then spreading warmth through her body. Benny stiffened, but she didn't bolt upright. Keeping her head enfolded in her arms, she waited. The touch moved up and down her back, then in circles. Soothing. Comforting. Like her mother did when she was small and so easily upset. It made her sniff back tears. It let her forget Dan and Henny. For now.

"Who—who are you?"

"August."

Not a voice. Not really. A sound inside her, making itself known.

"Why are you…contacting me?"

"You talk. I listen. You need a friend. So do I."

Lying on her belly was getting uncomfortable. Benny shifted. "I'm going to sit up. Okay?"

"Do as you wish, but I believe you must not look at me."

"Why?"

"I don't know. I only know when you do, I am pulled away."

"Okay. I won't look at you." Benny pushed herself upright, careful to keep her eyes on Henny's tombstone. She felt—August?—that presence off to her left. Shielding her periphery, she rested her elbows to her knees. "Is…was your name August?"

"I prefer Augie."

"Male or female?"

"Male."

"Are you buried here?"

"I am. I lived in this town for forty years."

"I've lived here all my life. Does your family still live in these parts?"

"They left long ago. We are forgotten here."

"This is so…wow. I have so many questions, my head is kind of spinning."

"Soon, but now, our time is short. Already it pulls me back."

"Back where?"

"Where I have been. You are the first. My first. I am not sure how all this works. I didn't know—"

"Didn't know what?" Benny lifted her head. "August? Augie?"

But she felt no presence. Chancing a glance out of the corner of her eye, she saw nothing. Her shoulders slumped. Not another car, scooter or bike awaited a rider. She was the only living soul in the cemetery. Pressing her palm flat to her husband's tombstone, she said, "I think I'm going nuts-o, Henny. What the hell is happening to me?"

That warmth returned to her shoulder. No presence. No sound inside her making itself heard. Just the warm sensation proving she wasn't alone. Benny lifted her hand from the granite marker. It trembled, but she moved it slowly, touching the spot to make sure it was real.

"Augie?"

The warmth gripped, like a hand grasping hers.

* * * *

"That was fast."

"But I did it, Harriet. Do you think I frightened her?"

"Nah. Not that one. She's been waiting all her life for a man like you."

"I am glad to see your sense of humor isn't as decayed as your corpse."

"Be nice, Augie, or I won't let you in on a little secret about being dead."

"I am nice. What secret?"

"You're working too hard at it."

"At being dead? I assure you, I'm having no trouble with—"

"Not that, you ninny. I mean you're pushing the boundary too hard, that's why it keeps pulling you back. Just be."

"Just be? What does that mean?"
"Try it next time, and you'll see."

* * * *

Bitterly Cemetery was big enough to make checking each headstone for the name *August* daunting. Asking Charlie to let her into the archives was a waste of time. The cemetery wasn't computerized and sifting through probably nonexistent old files was even more daunting than walking the whole thing. She'd see if it happened again first. Then, if she wasn't nuts-o, she would ask Augie himself where his final resting place was.

Only he wasn't resting.

Benny tucked the hair coming lose from her ponytail behind her ear. It was at that too long to leave loose at work, too short to put up length. Annoying, to say the least. Growing it out always seemed like a good idea, until it reached this point and she chopped it into a bob to tease at her chin. Her mother always claimed the fashion magazines said tall, curvy girls should not wear their hair short.

"You're far away, sugar."

Benny turned to the familiar drawl, a smile coming to her lips. Savannah took the clippers from her hand.

"Why don't you go to my office, rest a spell."

"Again?" Forced laughter trembled. Benny cleared her throat. "I'm not tired. Just preoccupied."

"You have been preoccupied since the day I met you," Savannah said. "I believe it must be your natural state."

"I used to daydream." Benny hung her head. "Now it's more like nightmares all the time."

Savannah bundled her into a hug. "You need a break. To my office with you. No sass-back. I'll bring you tea. We'll have a cup together."

"Herbal," Benny tossed over her shoulder as Savannah gently shoved her in the direction of her office. Grateful for the whining air conditioner perched in the window, Benny slumped into the comfy office chair rather than on the cot where her boss sometimes slept during lambing season. She breathed deeply, collecting thoughts before any more escaped.

Savannah pushed through the door, and set a cup of fragrant tea down on the desk. "You okay, Benny?"

"I keep telling you, I'm fine."

"And I keep not believing you."

Benny chuckled softly into her mug. Smart woman. But she took the opportunity as it came. "I'm thinking about taking a trip. Getting out of Bitterly for a while."

"Oh? When?"

"After Labor Day, don't worry."

"I wasn't. Where are you thinking about going?"

"North Carolina, to see my brother Tim and his family. I just feel like… like I have to get out of here."

"I couldn't agree more."

"Really?"

Savannah tucked the same escaped lock of hair behind Benny's ear. "Home and family can be as smothering as comforting," she said. "And I don't just mean your mother. I mean every little familiar thing here. They remind you, and keep you locked in a place you no longer know how to get out of, with memories that hold you back."

Benny sipped her tea. The kinship between them had always been natural, and only now did she wonder why when Savvy was tough as a steel-toed leather boot, and Benny was soft as an over-worn ballet slipper. But they both loved the farm, and growing things and—

"Why did you come north?" Benny asked.

"That you're asking just now tells me you know."

"You lost someone you loved."

Savannah nodded.

"Who?"

"Everyone," she said. "We are talking about you, Benedetta, and how you need a change of scenery. Have you told your mother?"

"I haven't told anyone but you."

"Good. Don't tell anyone else until just before you leave. Bless her heart, but your mother will try to talk you out of it. You need to go. You need to find your happiness again."

Head bowed, Benny twirled her wedding ring around and around her finger. Happiness. She had moments of it, certainly—like her week with Dan, and when she imagined holding her baby, rocking him to sleep, even changing diapers. Yet…

"It makes me feel guilty to think about being happy," she said. "How can I ever be happy again when Henny's dead?"

"Denying yourself happiness doesn't bring him back to life. It only wastes yours." Savannah hugged her from behind the chair. "Listen to me, sugar, as one who has been where you are. There are victims, and there are survivors. You are a victim. I am a survivor. Do you see the difference?"

Benny leaned into her. How many times had she wished she were more like Savannah? Moving north, buying a farm, living all on her own without any help, she lived. Every moment of every day, she lived deep in the life she built for herself, by herself. It made Benny feel weak, and sad, and too many things she had no name for.

"You live for the future," she said. "I live in the past."

"I like that." Savannah straightened. "Very nicely put. And exactly right."

"Thank you," Benny said. "I—I'm trying."

Savannah patted her back. "Drink your tea. When you're done, I can use your help with the chickens."

Benny sipped her tea growing cold in the air-conditioned office. Savannah was right. She needed out of Bitterly. New environs and a step out of the sad and easy familiarity of her life would change things. Change them back. Her rebellious spirit had contented itself on a scooter and cut hair for six years. If Benny didn't feed it soon, it would wither away completely.

The bubbles screensaver popped up on Savannah's computer screen. They drifted through the Savvy's blog post about the wonders of composting, Savannah's smiling face, the pictures of the farm. Benny leaned in and shifted the mouse, banishing the bubbles. She clicked through the comments page, checked the stats. Pride welled. People were responding positively.

One man shared a recipe for heirloom tomato and watermelon salad. "August tomatoes are best, being the sweetest of the season. Just be sure to use either red wine vinegar or white balsamic to balance the sweet."

The comment gave Benny an idea. She clicked into the admin page, made the necessary changes and in moments, and the blog had a place to post recipes for all to share. She went back to the main-page, and there was the little ticky, ready to click. Cut, paste and *Tomato and Watermelon Salad* became the first of what she hoped would turn into pages of recipes. Benny smiled, clicked on the edit ticky and added *August* to the name of the recipe.

It had been the first month in Benny's favorite time of year, until it became the month Henny died. Now, maybe, August would come to have a happier meaning again. She blew a trembling breath into her mug. No one but she would know the homage she made, the bit of magic she worked. Maybe Augie was manifest of her need to step out of the familiar. Maybe he was loneliness, or her rebellious spirit poking back at her.

Or maybe there was something to him after all.

Chapter 4

The Dream That in Them Lies

Few summer nights warranted more than the ceiling fan in Bitterly, Connecticut, but the day had been humid and the wet feel to the air lingered in her apartment. After tossing for an hour, Benny finally turned on the window-fan to pull in the cool night air. She stood in the generated breeze, nightgown billowing. The noise drowned out the night sounds she loved, but she had to work in the morning and doing so without sleep was not something her body could reconcile itself to these days.

Back between the sheets, Benny rolled onto her left side. According to the internet, it would increase the amount of blood and nutrients to reach her baby. Knees bent, a pillow between them, she was the model soon-to-be mother.

Less than five months to go.

The obstetrician at the childbirth clinic in East Perry gave her a November 14th due date, a sample bottle of vitamins, and an appointment schedule she had yet to keep. It took forever to get there on her scooter, and asking her mother for the car was tricky, at best. Clarice would ask to come, then pepper her with a thousand questions when Benny told her no. During the first trimester, when she still tried to convince herself it wasn't real, it didn't seem to matter. But she'd been feeling something lately, a fluttering. Quickening, the internet said. She liked that word much better. It sounded ancient and magical and like it was time to get back to the clinic.

Peter?

Yes, she would ask to borrow his car. He would be satisfied with her claim she was going to the mall up in Lee. She and Tim and all their friends used to do that as kids. She would call in the morning and make an appointment. Satisfied, sleepy thoughts rode the whir of the fan out of memory. The mall. Old friends she saw almost daily. Old friends she hadn't seen since high school. Tim. And Henny. Always Henny…

* * * *

And then they are sitting on a picnic table, leaning back on their hands, arms crisscrossed. Her head nestles onto his shoulder. His cheek rests on her hair. The ripped jeans Benny has on haven't fit in decades. She is wearing high-top Keds. Black, of course. She always wears black, these days.

"I'm sorry I didn't get to see you today," she tells him. "I had to help Savvy with the chickens."

"It's okay. I'm not there, anyway."

She lifts her head from his shoulder but does not look at him. "Then where are you?"

"I'm here. With you. In this place."

"Don't tease me." Now she does look. He is Henny. Her Henny as he was in his teens. She smiles. "Look at all your hair."

He ruffles the bangs. His eyes are bright and grey as a storm cloud. "Mom says I look like the Shaggy Detective."

"She wants you to buzz it, like Tim's."

"Tim's a jock."

"And you are not. You're not gothboy, either."

"No. I'm dead."

Benny startles, pulls back. Henny is no longer a moptop teenager. His eyes do not shine. His body is broken. His face like ash and hair matted with dried blood, he stares open-mouthed.

"Damn you," Benny screams. "If you'd been wearing your helmet—"

"How could you, Ben? With Dan? He was my best friend."

"Don't you dare! It's been six years."

"Six years is not forever. You promised me forever."

"Henny." Benny sobs. "Please. Please don't do this. I love you. I miss you."

He slides off the picnic table. "There is nothing here," he tells her. "No happiness. No sadness. Just…nothing."

Henny ambles away. He looks over his shoulder, once again the teenager she remembers so well. "It's not me. It's you. I'm sorry, Benny."

Reaching, sobbing, Benny cannot move. She is stuck to the picnic table, glued, stapled, stitched. She calls for him, but Henny is gone.

* * * *

Benny sobbed herself awake, sobbed his name over and over again. No. It couldn't be Henny saying such things. He wouldn't. Ever. She tossed aside the sheets, leapt out of bed, pulled her hoodie over her nightgown and slid her feet into her clogs. Hurried, careful, she went silently down the back steps. Helmet on, she got on her scooter and let it coast down the driveway. Only when she was on the street did she start it up.

Bitterly slept. All of it. No lights in any house but the occasional motion-sensors coming on as she passed. Through the quiet town with its faux gaslights gleaming, down South Main to the cemetery, she got off the scooter, moved the chain that had never kept her out as a kid, and would not do so now.

Benny left her scooter in the usual spot and trudged up the little hill to Henny's grave. She kissed her fingers and touched it to Mrs. Farcus' headstone as she passed, but spared no word for her old friend.

Moonlight turned Henny's stone white. In daylight, it was the same storm cloud gray of his eyes. Benny moved carefully, frightened for the first time in her life to be in the cemetery after dark. Her dream evoked skeletal hands popping out of graves, grabbing her ankles and dragging her underground. As a kid, it would have excited her, and more than a bit. Now, Henny's ashen face, the blood matting his hair, and words of his nothing-world robbed all such childhood thrill with the stark reality of her life.

By night, most of the garden flowers were closed. To Benny, they looked twisted inside-out rather than peacefully sleeping. Or it could have been the dream talking. Gathering her courage, she lowered herself to the dew-wet ground. She pushed fingers into dirt, hoping for the familiar comfort and not a skin-crawled shiver. Benny closed her eyes, sighing relief. She left her hands buried in her garden, in the sleeping flowers covering her husband's grave.

"I know it was a dream," she said. "You'd never scare me, or try to make me sad. But I felt you. I did. And now I can't remember anything but the bad part." She pulled her hands from the dirt. "I'm just so lost, Henny. For the last six years, I just went through my days. There wasn't any real happiness, but I didn't wallow in…"

No happiness. No sadness…It's not me. It's you.

"Did I do that, Henny? Did I ruin our time together? I'm sorry. I'm so sorry."

Tears, silent and painful. Benny eased onto her side—her left side—and rested her head in the crook of her shoulder.

"I'm not stupid." She coughed, waited for the tickle to subside. "I have lived in limbo since you died. In February, I took a step out of it and now that limbo won't let me back in. What did I do, Henny? What the fuck did I do? I don't want to live if living is without you."

"Language, Benedetta. But if what you say was true, you'd never have stepped out of your limbo. You'd never have taken the chance."

Benny came up on her elbow. "Augie?"

"Don't look!"

"I remember." In her periphery, Benny imagined some kind of glow. "How…how are you?"

"Dead. Much the same as I was." He laughed, a sound like leaves skittering, then, "And how are you, Benedetta?"

Benny gasped. "You…you suddenly sound different. Like a real voice."

"Ah, then Harriet was right."

"Harriet? As in…?"

"Your friend. Mrs. Farcus."

Benny resisted the urge to turn her head. "Is she…here?"

"No," Augie said. "She's still there. I'm not certain where I am. It is not where she is, and it is not where you are. I've been trying to reach this place, though. I think."

"You really never have done this before."

"No. And I don't have much of an idea how I'm doing it now. Harriet said, *just be.* That is what I am doing. I'm being."

Knees drawn to her chest, Benny rested her chin to them. "Mrs. Farcus. Harriet." She sniffed, wiped her drying tears. "This is all very strange, Augie. I'm inclined to think I'm asleep in the cemetery, dreaming on my husband's grave."

"Then let us make it a good dream, shall we?"

"I'd appreciate it. I just had a really bad one."

"About your husband, Henderson."

"Henny," she corrected. "He hated to be called Henderson. Yeah, about him. He…you sure he's not here? Or where Mrs. Farcus is?"

"I'm sorry, but yes, I am sure. Only me. Only Harriet. I am stuck here. She chooses to remain. Bitterly is where her soul belongs."

"Then there is something to heaven and hell. To souls and all."

"I couldn't say now any more than I could when I was alive and very Catholic. If there is a God and a Devil, I've never met them. I've come to understand that humans try very hard to explain the inexplicable, and often fail miserably. *Just be*, Harriet says. It is good advice, don't you think?"

Benny giggled. "Maybe she is God."

"You could be right. I am certain she is eavesdropping. She will let me know."

"Then…she hears me when I talk to her?"

"She says she has been listening to you since you were a child."

"That's so cool. How about you?"

"How about me, what?"

"How long have you been listening to me ramble to the tombstones?"

Augie didn't answer.

"Augie? Are you still there?"

"I am here. I…I don't know how to answer you. Time…it is not…I don't know how to explain it. It does not exist, at least, not in the same way. I have never thought about it before. Or maybe I have. I don't remember. I have been so long in that other place, or perhaps it's only moments."

"Do you remember the year you died?"

"I died. And now I'm here. And there is someone named Harriet…"

"Yes, Harriet Farcus. Is something wrong?"

"I…I do not know."

"Just be," Benny suggested. "Like Harriet said."

Her lower back had begun to ache. Between her and the wet, cold ground was a thin layer of cotton nightgown. While she waited for Augie to reorient himself, Benny unzipped her hoodie, slipped her arms free and laid it out on the ground. The faded and long-since retired Grim Reaper logo, only discernable for her love of the character and her memories, grinned up at her. Tim had gotten her the hoodie for Christmas when she was sixteen, even though he teased her for her style sense, or lack thereof. As if Tim knew anything about style with his unwavering choice of polo shirts and cargo pants.

On her back, arms behind her head, she kept her eyes on the stars swirling in an eternal sky above just in case Augie was still there. She shivered without the warmth of the hoodie on her bare skin. Gooseflesh prickled up the back of her neck, tightened her nipples uncomfortably. Benny palmed them for warmth.

"Do not cover up on my account."

Her eyes widened and she almost looked August's way. "I thought you were gone."

"Ah, no. Just being, as you suggested. And enjoying the view."

Benny's cheeks warmed, but she smiled discreetly.

"So…you can see me?"

"Of course."

"But I can't see you."

"It seems to be the way of it."

"That's hardly fair."

"Neither is it fair for you to be alive and lovely and for me to be dead and unable to show my appreciation for your…loveliness."

Benny let go of her breasts. If he could see her, he could also see how thin her nightgown was, and that she wasn't wearing underwear. A grin itched at her lips. It lit the smallest bundle of kindling under the young woman who would have lifted the bit of cloth away to stand naked in the moonlight in the event it were possible to seduce a ghost. With a slightly sad but almost satisfied sigh, Benny sat up and put the hoodie back on. "I should get home," she said. "I must seem a crazy person, lying in the grass, in a cemetery, talking to a ghost."

"I am the ghost, and the only one who knows you are doing so. But it is not good for a young woman to be wandering about so late at night, in so secluded a place. Bad things can happen."

"This is Bitterly." She zipped her hoodie up to the neck. "If you lived here, you know better. Nothing bad ever happens."

"Not true, Benedetta. When I was a young man, a girl was murdered. Beaten horribly and then drowned in the river."

"That's not true."

"It is true. Her name was Matilda Tully."

"Matilda?" Benny gasped. "As in Tilly?"

"I do believe she was called Tilly. Yes, Tilly Tully. I was a newcomer to Bitterly compared to my wife's family. At the time and never actually knew her. Why? Was she a relative of yours?"

"No, but there's a rock along the river, just north of town, called Tilly Rock, named for a girl who drowned. You can't be a kid in Bitterly without being dared to swim to it."

"And did you take such a dare, Benedetta?"

"Of course. It's just a story."

"Indeed it is, but your story is wrong. A girl was murdered by a spurned lover, her father blamed until they found her shoes hidden under the floorboards of her lover's house. Her father was released, but the man was never apprehended."

"Her shoes?" Goosebumps rose on Benny's arms. "This is really…I wonder if…"

"You wonder if what?" he asked.

Prickles of electricity were crackling up Benny's spine now. She stood up, clutching her hoodie closer. "Do you remember when she was killed?"

Augie was silent a moment, then, "I believe it was October. Yes. Before Halloween. No children were allowed to tricks-or-treats that year."

"I never put it together before," she said. "No one talks of the murder anymore, but it's a Bitterly-thing to put shoes out on the front porch every Hunter's Moon. That's the full moon in October. One person a year will find something in them. Pebbles, feathers. Nothing valuable or anything. I always thought it was just a fun tradition."

"We Italians have a tradition of leaving shoes on the stoop at Little Christmas, so *la Befana* can leave presents in them."

Benny laughed softly. "I know the tradition. My mother's Italian. But this is different. Only one person ever finds anything in their shoes, and I've heard lots of stories about parents putting stuff in their kids' shoes only to find whatever was in there gone in the morning. I wonder if it's Tilly."

"There was no such tradition while I lived in Bitterly."

"Well, if it came about because of her, there wouldn't be, would there." Benny thumbed her lip. She hadn't thought about the Halloweeny tradition in ages. It was probably nothing. Or maybe it wasn't. Later, she would consider how deep her nuts-o-ness went. Now, she just let it be.

"Go home, Benedetta, before you become a story children dare one another with."

"I'll go home," she said, "because I feel better now, and I'm tired, and I still have to work in the morning. Thank you, Augie."

"It is my pleasure. It is good to speak with someone who is not Harriet. She can be cantankerous."

"Tell her hi for me, okay?"

"I will."

Benny started away, then, "Can you show me where you are buried?"

"Come back tomorrow," he said. "I will try."

Nodding, she peeked out the corner of her eye. Augie? Or moonlight? Benny walked down the hill without looking back, without saying goodbye to Henny, or touching a kiss to Mrs. Farcus' tombstone.

* * * *

"Well?"

"Well what, August?"

"You were listening. I know you were."

"Then why are you asking?"

"I wasn't asking if you were listening, Harriet, you cantankerous witch, but what you thought about what you heard."

"I didn't like when you got naughty."

"I seem to recall being the naughty sort. I am closer to who I was in life when I am with her."

"Then you were no gentleman."

"Gentlemen don't have as much fun, Harriet. I...I don't quite understand what happened. I became so muddled. I didn't even tell her why I sought her out."

"*Do you remember why now?*"

"*The promise I made to my daughter, and didn't keep. I need Benedetta to help me keep it. Why could I not remember that, when I was with her? Why only here?*"

"*Here, there is no place to hide, Augie. Back there, closer to life? People hide from the truth all the time.*"

"*Like I hid my child in Italy from Katherine.*"

"*There you have it. Just understand this, August. Hard as it is to hold onto a dream after waking, once you speak it aloud, there is no forgetting again.*"

"*Is that what we are? Dreams?*"

"*Kind of like, I 'spect.*"

"*I don't think the living have any idea how very complicated death actually is, Harriet.*"

"*You got the right of it, Augie. The absolute right.*"

Chapter 5

The Sunset Hills

Benny checked the time again. Four o'clock. Still too early to skip out of work, even though she was finished with all Savannah asked her to do. She was actually feeling good today. No nausea at all. Her groin stitched now and again, those stretching ligaments and muscles were her newest reminder of the baby growing inside. Benny was actually looking forward to the doctor visit she had scheduled, including an ultrasound, as long as Peter let her borrow the car.

Gardening gloves stowed in her greenhouse cubby, along with her hand-trowel and rake, she took the garden debris out to the compost barrel and gave it a spin. Savannah had been out in the store a little while ago. Maybe she needed some help. It was the least Benny could do, considering the only appointment she was able to get was for Wednesday, the one day a week Savvy took off like it was a religious holiday. Hope as she might for the secret and sexy rendezvous Savannah needed, Benny acceded to the facts. Through all the years of their friendship, the only men in Savannah's life had been Edgardo and Raul, brothers from Ecuador and foremen at the farm. The notion of her boss and one of her foremen making her shudder and laugh at the same time, Benny almost missed spotting Dan getting out of his truck just as she turned the corner. She ducked, feeling foolish, but her heart hammered too fast to do anything but hide.

"Good afternoon, Daniel." Savannah's smooth drawl carried. Benny peeked around the corner of the farmstand.

"Afternoon, Savannah." Dan touched his brow like the country gentleman he was. "Got any of those striped tomatoes yet?"

"Not yet. But I do have some gold Brandywines."

"Sweet?"

"Like sugar."

"Great, thanks. I'll take two. Basil?"

"Always."

"Now if you have some of that soft farm cheese, I'm set for dinner."

"Of course I do. It's in the fridge."

Savannah led Dan into the store. Benny took slow, even breaths in a failed attempt to ease her heart rate. She counted to ten then made a dash for her scooter. Savannah would understand. If she knew. Which she didn't. Benny kicked the starter.

"No. No-no-no! Not now!" She kicked again. No hair-dryer-engine *bzzzz*. Dan's deep voice rumbled in her belly, got louder. Closer. Benny gave it all she had. The engine sputtered to life. She twisted the throttle and spun gravel out of the parking lot.

Sorry, Savvy. She threw the thought over her shoulder, but did not look back to see if they were both watching her zip away like a crazy person. Tears dried almost instantly, and Benny realized she hadn't grabbed her helmet. Fear welled up worse than any nausea she'd felt these past months. How did she forget her helmet? Her damned helmet.

The engine sputtered. The scooter slowed, bucked, and turned off. Benny coasted to the side of the road, put her head in her arms and sobbed. In the darkness behind her lids, the nightmare image of Henny's broken body formed. She held onto that ghastly image until she could no longer do so without screaming.

Benny wiped her eyes, sniffed. She unscrewed the gas cap, gave the scooter a shake. No swoosh. No gas. She almost laughed, but feared it would start her crying again. She moved the scooter farther to the side and lowered the kickstand. A vehicle pulled over. She knew who it was without looking.

"Hey, Dan."

"Need some help?"

"Out of gas. You wouldn't have any in the truck, would you?"

"Sorry, no. But I got some planks back there. I can get the scooter in the bed and drive you home."

The jaw-watering sensation that had nothing to do with her pregnancy and everything to do with the sickening feeling she would vomit any second kept her silent. She only nodded and got into the truck. He wouldn't have let her help him anyway.

Sunshine came through the window. Shielding her eyes, Benny lowered the visor. The mirror there reflected Dan in the truck bed. His shirt stretched taut across his broad back. Sunlight caught out the blond of his younger days, now turned a shade or two darker. He squinted against the sunlight as he struggled the scooter into the truck bed, brow furrowed. Taller than most men she knew, he was one of the few in town she didn't tower over. Benny had liked that about him, during the week of happiness she stole from him. She liked too much about him, and that was the problem in a nutshell.

"I only had one webbing strap," he said as he got into the truck, "but it should be fine for the short ride to your place."

"Thanks."

He glanced up from fastening his seatbelt. "You okay? You look like you're going to be sick."

"You have that effect on me." She tried to laugh, but it came out as a bark.

"I figured as much, the way you been acting since Valentine's Day." But he smiled when he said it, and Benny felt a little better. He turned in his seat. "Listen, Benny, it didn't work out. I won't say it didn't break my ornery old heart a bit, but I been alone a long time. Probably always will be. We were friends a long time before we were anything else. Can't we be again?"

Benny's shoulders slumped. Her head told her to tell him. Now was the perfect time. Her throat and tongue and mouth had other ideas. Again, she nodded. He waited then, letting go a deep and exasperated breath, Dan turned over the engine and pulled back onto the road.

The drive into town was silent, and only when they passed the cemetery did Benny remember Augie's request for her return. In truth, she didn't have it in her. All she wanted was her stuffy apartment, a shower, and the television remote.

Dan turned into her driveway and pulled around back, hopped out of the truck and rolled her scooter from the bed. Benny made a half-hearted attempt to help him but he waved her away. He wheeled it into the space under the steps as if he knew exactly where she kept it, as of course he did, because she had told him the night of their carriage ride, and Dan Greene remembered.

"You have a can? I'll pick up some gas for you."

"It's okay," she said. "I keep a full can in the shed. The scooter gets such good gas mileage I forget it ever needs to be filled."

"It's not a bad problem to have." He jutted his thumb at his truck. "That thing guzzles gas like a frat-boy at a kegger."

Benny smiled, but she didn't laugh. Dan's smile faded. He looked down at his hands, fingers spread wide, then turned them over. The backs were freckled, his arms covered in fine, blond hair, so pale in the sunshine. A momentary and quickly suppressed sensation of those arms around her, pulling her close, made her take a step back. He reached out as if to catch her, but Benny put up her hands.

"What did I do, Ben?" he asked so softly. "Whatever it was, I didn't mean it."

"I have to go inside," Benny turned away but he caught her hand. She stared at it. The words came out of her mouth before she could stop them. "I'm seeing someone."

"Oh."

"His name is…is August. I only met him recently."

"I see." He still had her hand. Benny wanted to take the words back. She wanted to so badly.

"Dan, I—"

"Forget it," he said, letting go her hand and taking a step back. "It was…I was…anyway."

"Yoohoo, Daniel!"

Clarice Grady stepped onto the porch landing, her gaze going from one to the other and her face instantly brightening.

"What brings you here on this lovely day?"

Benny rolled her eyes.

"Hello, Mrs. Grady. Just helping Benny. She ran out of gas."

"Benedetta, that blasted scooter again?"

"I ran out of gas, Ma. It happens."

"Since you're here, Daniel, I'm RSVPing to Mabel's graduation party." Clarice's gaze flicked to Benny. "We'll be there. All of—"

"I'm going up," she cut in. "Dan, thanks for the lift."

"You're welcome," he said, far more softly than he should have in Clarice's hearing. Benny hurried up the back steps, slamming the door a little too hard. Her mother would invite Dan to dinner. He would refuse, of course, especially after the lie she told, but what if he didn't? She yanked open the refrigerator door, unsurprised by the cold air and a lot of nothing blasting her in the face, and closed it again. When had she actually gone grocery shopping last? Thirty-six years old and she still ate most of her suppers with her family downstairs in the kitchen she'd been eating meals in most of her life. When she and Henny shared this space, she cooked like her mama cooked and loved doing it. Benny shopped—always local—and made everything from scratch. It was her joy, not her chore. Henny died and took that joy from her too.

"Damn you," she grumbled. "Damn you and what you did to me. To my life. How could you?"

A knock lifted her head. Clarice waved from the half-glass door. Benny let her in.

"It's not locked."

"I didn't want to intrude."

"You?" Benny chuckled. She kissed her cheek. "What's up, Ma?"

Clarice stepped into the apartment and closed the door behind her. She pushed a stray curl from her forehead. "Daniel went home," she said.

"Okay. And?"

"And?" Clarice fumbled, her color rising. "What's going on with you two, sweetheart? You seemed to have a good time together last winter. The carriage ride and—"

"I don't want to talk about Dan."

"Is it Henny?"

"I don't want to talk about him either. Just let it go, Ma. This is my mess to figure out."

Clarice cocked her head. "Mess?"

Benny closed her eyes, gritted her teeth. "I said let it go. I mean it."

The couch in her small sitting room beckoned. Benny flopped into it and clicked the television on. Flip, flip, flip. Nothing but news, kiddie-tv and old sitcoms. Her mother sat down beside her. She said nothing, only took Benny's hand and traced her knuckles. A familiar touch, one tugging at the bindings trussing Benny up. Loosening them. Without meaning to, Benny slumped into her mother, rested her head to her soft shoulder, and wept.

"You just cry, baby," Clarice smoothed her hair. "Just cry."

Benny let go. It felt good to be held like a little girl crying tears over nothing more dire than a lost plaything or a tiff with a school friend. Her mother stroked her hair, whispered soothing sounds. She asked no questions and offered no advice, and for this, Benny loved her so much.

"I'm tired of being sad," she said finally.

"It has been too long, Benny. It's time to let him go. To be happy again."

Benny sat up. She took the crumpled tissue her mother handed her and blew her nose. "I know," she said. "But it makes me feel so horrible to even consider being happy. I just don't know what to do."

"Can I ask you a question you're not going to like?"

"Is it about Dan?"

Clarice nodded.

"Fine, Ma. Ask."

"Did he make you happy, last winter?"

"Yes."

"Okay, baby." Clarice rose to her feet, kissed her daughter's head. "You coming down to dinner? I'm making pork chops."

Benny wiped her nose again, cocked her head. "That's it?"

"Roasted potatoes, too. And green beans. They aren't as wonderful as the ones Savannah will have in—"

"That's not what I meant and you know it."

Her mother smiled, thumbed a tear from Benny's cheek. "I know, sweetheart. Dinner's at six thirty."

Her mother left her sitting alone and stunned. Disbelief and relief vied for first place in Benny's head. She dabbed her face dry, tried blowing her nose on the tissue one time too many and ended up a mess. Washing her hands, she smiled wryly. Between a ghost chatting her up and her mother keeping her thoughts to herself, the ghost was far, far less strange.

* * * *

He tried being angry, the whole ride driving home. Dan Greene was sorry. Sorry Benny's grief was still so raw. Sorry he'd moved too fast. Sorry she—they all—lost Henny, period. He couldn't go past the place where his friend died without getting choked up. Being a first responder on the scene had been the stuff of nightmares, the kind that often appeared in his sleep. It was nothing short of miraculous Benny hadn't seen her husband twisted and bloody and broken. Her scooter usually kept her to the confines of Bitterly, but she had gone to a baby shower in Great Barrington. An old high school friend, if he remembered right. By the time he, Tim and Charlie took her to the site, the clean-up crew had done a good job of clearing it all away. Someone left a bouquet tied to a tree. He remembered Benny taking it down, picking out the dead flowers and bringing the rest home.

Henderson Parker Fredricks, you moron. You stupid, careless moron. How could you do that to her? To all of us? Idiot.

Henny, Tim, Charlie and Dan. The wild one, the jock, the nice guy, and the comedian. Best buds. Dan couldn't remember a time they'd not been friends, and always figured it started in kindergarten. At Henny's funeral, he learned it went even further back, almost to the womb and the momentarily trendy "Expecting Club" their mothers had been members of. They were boys born and raised in Bitterly. Men who never left. Until Tim, after Henny died and proved there was no such thing as 'all the time in the world.'

Instead of passing by the cemetery, Dan pulled in. He hadn't been there since the February prior. Valentine's Day, in fact. Finding Henny's grave was easy enough. Benny made it so.

He spotted the matching gardens—Henny's, and the woman whose name he never remembered. It always made him smile to recall the goth phase Benny went through, believing she had a connection to the woman resting there more than a hundred years. Tim teased her mercilessly back then. Benny never got angry or upset. Their bond and understanding was that absolute. Tight as he and Evelyn were since their parents' deaths, it wasn't anything like Tim and Benny. There were years when Dan would have gladly not seen his sister for more than the holidays, like most of those years during her marriage to Paul.

He trudged up the hill, squatted at the garden-graveside. He traced the letters on the stone, as if it would somehow conjure Henny from the dead. Benny would have the words to say, brought back from those teen years of pagan rituals she had been so serious about. He wondered if she'd tried them after Henny died, for old-time's sake. Or desperation.

"Remember when we were kids?" he asked the air. "And Tim dared you to kiss his sister. I thought it was a bad idea. So did Charlie. I think Tim must have known what he was doing though, considering how he was with her. You remember. He could tease her all he wanted but anyone else who did paid the price."

Dan laughed softly. He plucked a few dead leaves from the marigolds.

"You came back and got your five bucks for doing the deed, but everything changed. Not that any of us knew, back then. *She got under my skin,* is what you told me after I asked why you were hanging out with her instead of us. I never got it, Henny. Girls. Women. I saw my dad smack my mom around and never got why she didn't toss his ass out. Then my sister with Paul. Damn idiot, she is. Was. I never got that under-your-skin feeling for anyone. But Benny?" He chuffed. "She's way under. I never told her I asked you if it was okay that I take her out. I was afraid she'd think it was creepy. Maybe I should have. Told her, I mean. Not that you answered me. You and me, we were tight. Better was me than some other asshole, right?"

Dan chuckled softly, fought the tightening in his throat.

"Now she's making up a boyfriend. How's that for a do not disturb sign? I think he's pretend, anyway. If you got any sway in things, I'd sure appreciate some help."

Dan rose to his full height and brushed his hands clean. Colorful and profuse, the garden was nevertheless as safe as it was pretty. Pansies and marigolds. Forget-me-nots and snapdragons. Only annuals that didn't have to survive harsher weather, never any perennials that did. As a landscaper, it had struck him as strange Benny would only plant flowers requiring a complete re-do, year after year. As a man who cared for her—and a smarter one than most gave him credit for—Dan understood all too well.

Chapter 6

A Silken Skirt of Breeze

A full tank of gas, jeans, a high-necked T-shirt and the faithful Grim Reaper hoodie for when it got cooler, Benny went to the cemetery prepared this time. In the milk crate she had a sandwich, a thermos of lemonade, and an old blanket to sit on. Despite the prior night's provocative comment, or perhaps because of it, Benny was looking forward to her visit with Augie. Maybe she was nuts-o. Maybe he was real. After tonight, she would have proof one way or the other. She would make sure of it.

Riding through town, Benny didn't resist the urge to stop in CC's for something sweet to go with her otherwise non-exciting dinner. She pulled her scooter up onto the sidewalk where customers sat at the bistro tables. The weather was cool and dry, the air scented by sunshine and cut grass and the briar roses currently growing rampant along every rock wall and roadside. A welcome respite after a few days of humidity.

If you don't like the weather in New England, wait an hour.

"Jo? Anyone here?" Benny rang the bell on the counter. Nearly empty racks on the wall disheartened, until Benny spotted the tray of her favorite chocolate mud cookies.

"Oh, hey, Benny." Caleb, Charlie McCallan's middle son, came out of the back room with a broom. "I thought I heard the bell ring. Can I get you something?"

"A mud cookie. Make it two."

His face colored. "I'm supposed to bring two dozen over to a graduation party as soon as I close up, but I suppose Johanna wouldn't mind, seeing it's you."

Graduation party. Dan's niece. She'd forgotten all about it.

"No, no. Don't do that. How about one of those big tollhouse cookies instead?"

"You sure?"

"Positive. I was torn between the two anyway."

Caleb slid the cookie into a waxed-paper sleeve and set it on the counter. Benny handed him a dollar and took a bite.

"Didn't you graduate this year?" she asked him.

"Next year."

"You look into any schools yet?"

The cash drawer dinged closed. "I'm pretty set on going to the Culinary Institute, like my sister. I love working in the bakery. I can't imagine doing anything else."

"Fantastic, Caleb. Really great." Benny took another bite. "Johanna must be thrilled."

"Just a little." He grinned, and in that instant looked exactly like Charlie. "Charlotte wants me to come south for the summer."

"She really likes it down there in Cape May, huh?"

"Loves it."

"You going to go?"

He shrugged. "Maybe for a couple of weeks. I don't want to be gone all summer. It's my last one as a high school student. I kind of want to hang with my friends."

"She'll understand."

"This is Charlotte we're talking about."

"True." Benny put the last bite of cookie into her mouth. "I can't believe I just ate that whole thing. You'd better give me another. It was supposed to be for later."

* * * *

Her cookie tucked safely into the milk crate, Benny zipped out of town. It would remain light for a while yet. She had time to visit and still be able to get home before dark. She wasn't a teenaged-goth-chick anymore. There was only so much time she could spend casually hanging out in the cemetery before other people started questioning her sanity.

Scooter parked, she gathered her picnic supper from the milk crate. Henny's plot looked pretty from a distance. Welcoming. Harriet's too. Benny laid her blanket between the two, put her food on it, and went first to her husband's grave. A hand placed upon the stone, she bowed her head and searched for words that never sufficed even if she did find them. The dream still spooked her. It hadn't been the first time her Henny turned into zombie-Henny within the confines of her mind. All the other times, she woke in a cold sweat. This time he'd spoken—*It's not me. It's you. I'm sorry, Benny*—and his words spooked her more than his altered form.

Letting her hand fall, Benny turned to Mrs. Farcus's grave instead.

"It's no use. I'm a mess."

Nothing.

"Augie asked me to come back. He said he'd show me where he's buried. Anyone there? Augie? Mrs. Farcus?" She swallowed hard. "Harriet?"

Still nothing. She went back to her blanket, sat down, and opened her sandwich. The giant cookie had robbed her appetite. She ate anyway, washed it down with the lemonade. The second cookie taunted her. She picked it up, nibbled at the edge.

"I am eating for two, you know," she told it, and ate the whole thing. If she couldn't have one of Johanna's mud cookies, two of her tollhouses were ample compensation. She felt a wee bit queasy, though she licked her fingers clean. Leaning back on her elbows, she looked up at the darkling sky. If she wanted to get home before dark, she had to leave soon.

She rose groaning to her feet, gathered the garbage, and started for her scooter. Stopping at Harriet's grave, she noted a few marigolds ruining the orange and yellow tableau with their withered brown-ness. Benny deadheaded them, grimaced at a bare spot she hadn't noticed before. She would bring something to fill it with, next time she visited.

"I guess I've been stood up," she said, brushing her hands clean and re-gathering her garbage. "Could you tell him I was here? Augie, I mean. Not Henny. I'm pretty certain he's not here. Not like you, or Augie. Hell, I don't even know if you are here or I'm just wishing so hard that—"

The cookie wrapper whipped out of her hand and fluttered away. Benny grabbed for it. It dodged. It actually dodged. She dropped the rest of her what she still held and she gave chase. The wrapper caught on a tombstone, a tuft of grass, a branch, a bouquet of flowers long-since wilted, skipping, lifting, rolling on a non-existent breeze Benny wouldn't think about until she caught it, lest she think too hard and decide she was completely nuts after all. She followed it all the way across the cemetery. It obliged by waiting until she caught up, winded and slightly annoyed to be chasing animated garbage. It finally splatted against the face of a tombstone, in an older area of the cemetery, and there stuck. Panting, Benny swiped it, and read:

Katherine Weller Fiore
September 13, 1919 ~ January 28, 1976
*

August Fiore
July 4, 1908 ~ July 7, 1980

Benny shoved the wrapper into her pocket. She knelt at the grave, traced his name with the tip of a trembling finger. Looking back the way she had come, she found no splash of color to mark Henny's grave. Beyond the row of tombstones, a wrought-iron fence, and trees dotted with lightning bugs. She rose and moved to the fence, gripping it with both hands, and remembered a summer evening like this one, when she was fourteen. These woods. On the other side of the fence. And Henny.

"On the dramatic side, but it worked."

She caught herself before spinning to his spectral voice. "Augie?"

"Who else would it be?"

"I hardly know anymore. You have no idea—"

"Hold that thought just a minute…"

A sensation like a breath gasped made Benny blink, but she didn't look at it.

"There," Augie said. "Is this better?"

Less spectral. More real. He was getting better at making the transition. Or she was only wishing. "I suppose," she said.

"Something wrong, Benedetta?"

Yes. No. "I'm assuming it was you, with the cookie wrapper?"

"It was. Impressed?"

"Annoyed is more like it. I'm not in the best shape for running across a cemetery."

"You look quite shapely to me."

"Stop that." She bit at the insides of her cheeks to keep from grinning. "Why didn't you just talk to me?"

"I haven't quite mastered moving from depth to depth yet. Forgive me, but it was easier to get you here this way."

"Depth?"

He chuckled. "My own notion, ah? The best way I can describe it is that going from the place I mostly exist in to here, where I am with you now is like kicking off at the bottom of a pool. It is fast, at first, and slows as I get to the top. From deep to shallow. From dark to light. That is why it's easier for me to move about when in the deep place. See?"

"Kind of. I guess. Not really."

"Well, you are here now. You wanted to see my grave. This is it."

Benny let it go and instead focused again on the marker, the names and dates there. "You were married."

"Katherine. Wonderful woman. Love of my life."

"Kids?"

"Two sons, Philip and Victor, and a daughter, Adriana."

"Where are they now?"

"They moved out of Bitterly a long time ago. And I am still here. Perhaps they, too, are no longer among the living."

"But your wife died before you did. Wasn't she waiting for you or anything?"

"No. She died a several years before I did, so—"

"So, then we don't all find one another after death."

"That, I cannot say. All I know is it is not so for me. Yet."

Benny bit her lip. She wanted this to be real so badly it made her teeth ache. Since Augie first tapped her shoulder, she had something to look forward to again. Weird, perhaps, but Benny once prided herself on weird. Was he real? Or was he wishful thinking gone haywire?

"Augie?"

"Yes, Benedetta?"

"I need something. Something physical."

"If I could do that for you, *cara mia*, I would be happy to oblige, but as far as I know, such a thing is not possible."

Benny bit the insides of her cheeks again. "You are a fiend."

"I think you like fiends."

She used to. Now she liked…

She cut off the thought before it fully formed. "I meant something physical as proof I've not lost my mind completely. Everything happening, even talking to you now, could be memory forcing itself out of my head. The woods right there"—she pointed beyond the wrought iron fence—"is where Henny kissed me for the first time. Maybe that's where I got your name from. Maybe I saw it all those years ago and now my grief is pulling it out of my brain. I need to know you're not a figment of my imagination."

"Sure, sure. Any ideas?"

"I was hoping you'd have one."

Benny paced, keeping the sense of him ever in her periphery. Perhaps because it was getting dark, there was something different in the glow she imagined him to be, tempting her to look. Was that shadow the faded image of an elbow? The slope of a hip? She squeezed her eyes shut tight. "You said you lived in Bitterly for forty years, right?"

"More or less."

"Did you do anything noteworthy that might have made the papers? Win some prize at the Fourth of July picnic, or save a puppy from drowning or something?"

"No, nothing like that."

"Hmm, well, maybe you took out a permit to put up a shed or something I could look up in the town records?"

"Permit for a shed? Ha! Benedetta, you could build a whole house in this town back then without a permit, and there were no building codes. I should know. I built my house from…"

"Augie?" She shielded her eyes as she spun to where she last heard his voice. "Are you there?"

"I am," he said. "I just remembered something, and if it's still there, it will give you the proof you wish."

* * * *

Benny switched the headlight of her scooter off as she rounded the corner of Division Street. When Bitterly was first founded, and the Green sat closer to the river, Division Street marked the middle between the northern and southern ends of town. Commerce wisely moved to higher ground after the annual flooding in 1855 devastated the town one time too many, taking the Green and municipal buildings with it. Now it was a strange name for a road out in the middle of nowhere, and clutching the past too determinedly to let go.

Three of the original structures survived—Bitterly Congregational Church, the Bossy House and the Weller house. Benny wondered if Augie's Katherine was one of the Wellers. Considering she and Augie had built their home on the same street as the original family homestead, she figured she must have been.

Benny's stomach flipped. Of all the houses in Bitterly, why did the one Augie build have to be 105 Division Street? Why couldn't it even have been one hundred eight, or two-eleven? Nope. One. O. Five.

Evelyn Taylor's house.

Dan's sister.

With whom he lived since her husband skipped town four years ago.

Of course, it was the house Augie built back in 1935. More proof it was all in her head. *Benedetta, you idiot.*

But she glided to a stop at the bottom of the drive, parked the scooter and took off her helmet anyway. During the week she stole from Dan, she had never once been in the house. Benny could count on one hand the number of times she had been on Division Street in her life. At least there was that in her favor if she found what Augie had sent her to find.

She skirted the shadows along the driveway, hunkered down behind the big rock with the house numbers on it. There were only two lights on inside—one upstairs and one in the back visible because of the picture window without curtains. The light went out. Moments later, another went on upstairs. Benny checked her watch. After eight o'clock. The party must have ended on the early side. Though she had come prepared to crash with apologies, she was happier skulking in like a thief.

She crept up the driveway and slipped around back. Even in the dark, the landscaping was lovely. Stone walls, not the farmer-walls cutting through every property in New England, but carefully constructed and meticulously placed stone walls, lined the yard. Plantings accented the walls. A grape arbor, heavily vined and currently lightning-bugged, stood back against the trees. Somewhere, lilies bloomed. Their scent was sweet, heady, and unmistakable. Benny sighed softly, bit her lip, and started her search for the proof Augie said would be just off the cellar doors.

* * * *

The sound of feet crunching on the gravel driveway lifted Dan's head. He listened, but it didn't come again. Instead of unbuttoning his jeans as he'd been about to do, he re-did the first one and headed downstairs barefoot.

He looked out the front window, then the back. Nothing but a quiet yard, and maybe deer. Pretty as the gardens were by day, Dan preferred them at night when all the night-bloomers popped. The hedge of four o'clocks, the evening primrose, night gladiolas, the copse of snow-white moonflowers and, his favorite, Casablanca lilies that cost him a small fortune his sister didn't know about.

Pride swelled. Winters in Bitterly were long and white. Plowing had always brought more money in than landscaping, but creating whole worlds in miniature, of color and scent with living plants and native stone, made him the artist he would never claim to be. The New Yorkers currently buying places in the country brought more work than he could handle this summer, and it wasn't even July yet. If Bitterly didn't depend upon him and his plow, Dan wouldn't even have to work next winter. It would be nice to spend the cold months scouring seed catalogs, maybe even building a greenhouse to—

Metal scraped on stone. Dan grimaced. Something was in the little alcove off the cellar. Raccoons after party leftovers that didn't get cleaned up, more than likely. Scaring them off was easy enough, but they'd be back as soon as the lights went out. Someone had to clean up whatever they were after. As always, that someone was him. Dan grabbed a garbage bag and went to investigate.

"Dammit!" A hissed whisper came from the alcove as he opened the back door. Not raccoons. He craned his neck. Big as he was, Dan Greene was no fool. Even Bitterly had its delinquents. Reaching slowly for the light switch just inside the door, he caught sight of the intruder's shadowed silhouette. And knew it instantly. Having memorized it one stunned and sleepless night watching her dream beneath the stars.

Dan treaded carefully. He didn't want to scare her off. She was sitting at the wrought iron bistro table, in a chair still tied up with balloons. Head in her hands and grumbling, she didn't hear him approach. Neither did she hear him clear his throat.

"You are not making all this up, Benedetta Marie Grady," she whispered harshly. "You are not losing it. You've believed in this shit all your life and now it's actually happening and—"

Dan stepped on what felt like a bottle cap. "Oh! Ow-ow-ow!"

Benny's head shot up.

Hopping on one foot, Dan caught her chair before she toppled. "Sorry, sorry!" He fought off the balloons. "I was trying not to startle you. Wasn't looking where I was going."

"Dan, I—I—I—hi."

Benny looked up at him, her eyes big as moons. He put his foot down gingerly.

"Hi." He wouldn't blink, afraid she would disappear if he did. "What are you doing here?"

Benny's head bowed, robbing him of those eyes.

Idiot. Wrong words. Fancy meeting you here? No. Dumb. You looking for me or trying to beat the raccoons to the pickin's? Dammit.

"You invited me to the party," she said. "Remember?"

"The party was over hours ago." *Dammit again.*

"I see that."

Silence fell and lingered. Benny's head didn't come up, but she didn't leave either. Dan steadied his heartbeat, and his hands, and thought about what Charlie might say, or even Tim. Just not Henny.

"You want a beer?" *Okay. Not bad.*

She lifted her head. "Beer? No, thanks."

"You want to come in? There's still some food left—"

"No. No, thank you." She stood up. The balloons hit Dan in the face. He batted them away and caught Benny trying not to laugh. She bit her lip. Adorably.

"Can I get some water?" she asked, pointing to the tub of melted ice where bottles of water and a few cans of soda bobbed. Dan grabbed one, wiped it dry on his shirt and handed it to her.

"Thanks." She cracked the cap. Dan tried not to stare at her lips on the mouth, at her throat as she swallowed. Benny gestured with the bottle. "It's really pretty back here. You did all this?"

"Mostly."

Benny took another sip. She fidgeted from foot to foot. "The walls?"

"Yup. Every rock."

"This patio?"

He tapped his bare foot on the pavers.

"This too. It used to be a concrete slab. The arbor is pretty much the only thing I didn't put in. It's been here since before Evelyn and Paul bought the place."

"It looks old."

"Probably almost as old as the house. Evelyn says a Weller girl married an Italian immigrant back during the Depression. He built this house. I bet he did the arbor too. I found a press and some old barrels in the cellar when I did the renovations for my apartment."

"Really?" The uncomfortable fidgeting vanished. A glimpse of the old Benny before the cloud of grief doused her shined out of her like moonbeams. "That doesn't sound like a Weller."

"I like to think she was a rebel. Evelyn says it's because the Italian was good-looking and had an accent."

"How does she know?"

"She doesn't. Wishful thinking."

Benny laughed. The sound reverberated in Dan's gut.

"So," she said, glancing at the ground, "this used to be a concrete slab?"

He pointed to the French Doors. "Those used to be old cellar doors too. You know, the kind that pull up? The foundation of the house is mostly stone and dirt. No rec-room for the—"

"The old patio isn't under this, is it?"

"No…why?"

Benny took a long swig of water. Something was up. After telling him she was seeing someone just the other day, she was suddenly sneaking into his yard, and it wasn't to discuss the landscaping. Dan crossed his arms, then uncrossed them before she noticed and took it the wrong way. *Cut it, tool-bucket. She's here. She's talking. Don't blow it.*

"The concrete was thick." He flexed like a muscle-man in an old comic advert. "Took days to break it up."

Benny rewarded him with a smile. A real smile. She sipped her water.

"Any bodies underneath?" she asked. "You know…Italian? 1930s? Maybe some mob connection."

"You're such a racist."

"I can't help it. It's the way I was raised."

Silence fell. The easy kind that came as naturally as the banter back and forth. She had been his best friend's kid sister, then his other best friend's wife, not a romantic interest, and thus a girl Dan never felt awkward around. It hadn't changed when his feelings for her did, and now the easy and natural banter coexisted as equal parts relieved and giddy. The warmth radiating up from his toes and out the top of his head made him feel like his hair was on fire. It took all his effort not to pat at it, just to be certain.

"This is going to sound strange," Benny said. "But were there... handprints in the concrete. Like, kids' handprints?"

Dan's belly lurched. "How did..." He shook it off. "Come with me."

"Huh?"

"Just come on."

Dan resisted the urge to hold out his hand for hers. She wouldn't take it, and he'd be a fool twice over. Instead, he led her to the detached garage, and switched on the light. He and Evelyn kept no cars in there, only his landscaping equipment, the plow for his truck, and the sleigh-cum-carriage he took out at Christmas for the sleigh-rides on the green. The same carriage he had taken Benny out in on Valentine's Day.

"Over there." He helped her navigate around and between things, taking her arm instead of her hand. The broken-off slab of cement leaned up against the far wall, just where it had been the last two years. Benny squatted down before it. She traced the initials—PF, VF, and AF—then the handprints. Dan squatted down just beside and behind her, his knee almost touching the small of her back.

The silence stretched while she stared, her fingers tracing and tracing as if trying to prove what she saw was real. Dan's knees began to ache, but he would not move, not when she was so close her flower scent made his head light, the heat of her body aroused. So close he could almost hear her thoughts.

"Why did you save this?" she asked without turning.

"I just couldn't do it," he said. "Tossing them out with the rest of the rubble? Just couldn't."

"That's really sweet." She glanced over her shoulder. "So unlike you, right?"

"Totally out of character."

"If only the world knew what an asshole you really are." They laughed together. Dan's knees popped as he rose. Benny stayed where she was.

"What are you going to do with it?" she asked.

"I wanted to work it into the pavers, but Evelyn thought it was creepy. I figure I'll hide it out beyond the arbor where she won't even notice it. Those little hands belong here, don't you think?"

Benny rose slowly to her feet. Dan reached to help her, and though she didn't need his help, she took his hand. Benedetta Marie Grady was flighty and whimsical, but she was not incapable even if her grief made her seem fragile. Dan knew better than to believe it, or wish it, for a second.

"I think they do, too," she answered. "Thanks for showing me."

"You'll keep my secret, right?"

"The secret from Evelyn about your sinister plan for the creepy handprints? Or the no-secret about you being such a mush?"

"Both."

"I'll do my best, but no promises."

"It's all I can ask."

He led her back through the obstacle course of his garage, closing the door softly behind them. Back in the night garden, she breathed deeply.

"I smell lilies."

Dan moved to his bed of Casablanca lilies and snapped one from its stem. He held it out to her. "Casablancas," he said. "I get them over at White Flower Farm, in Morris."

Her eyes met his. She took the lily, their fingers grazing and sending a jolt up Dan's arm. He rubbed at the hair suddenly standing on end.

"I love White Flower Farm," she said. "It's been years since I even thought about going."

"Probably since you started working at Savvy's."

"Yeah, you're probably right. She doesn't grow exotic plants, though. And it's hard to get there on my scooter."

Was she hinting? Dan cleared his throat. "Well, you should come with me next time I go."

"I'd like that."

Score! "They know me there. I get a discount."

"Or course you do." Benny sniffed at the flower. "Because you're such an asshole, I guess, they can't wait to get you off the premises."

"Must be it."

"Must be."

The easy silence settled over them, around them. Benny's smile didn't fade, but the longer the silence lingered, the more Dan felt the need to fill it.

"You sure you won't come in? There's a ton of food left over."

"No, thanks. It's getting late. I already ate, anyway."

"Let me walk you to your scooter then," he said. "Where'd you park it? I didn't hear you drive up."

"I'm just down the driveway. You have no shoes on. I think I can manage." Benny lifted the lily. "Thank you."

"You're welcome." Dan touched his eyebrow in a causal salute. "I guess I'll see you around, Benny."

She walked away, and Dan felt no desire to follow her even if his body would oblige, which it wouldn't. Whatever had just happened was enough. Perfect, even. The start he should have made back in February when he pushed too hard and scared her off. He stood beside the bed of lilies, listening. To the crunch of gravel. To the scooter revving to life. To the mechanical whine fading in the distance. Dan listened until there was nothing left to listen to but the night.

* * * *

Benny didn't go home. She needed some distance between Dan and slumber. It was a pattern established back in February, taking space between seeing him and going home where she and Henny had lived. This time, she went back to the cemetery, back to Augie's grave, but though she called and called to him, he didn't appear. Riding through the narrow lanes of this place so familiar, the scent of Dan's lily wafted, so heady it almost nauseated. As she walked up the hill to Henny's grave, she plucked the flower from its place in the buttonhole of her shirt, twirled it between two fingers. The pale stamens and filaments were, in sunlight, pale green, but in moonlight as white and translucent as the petals. A smile came unbidden to her lips and for once, Benny didn't squelch it.

Though habit sent her first to Henny, her husband definitely was not frequenting the cemetery where she had interred his mortal remains. If ever she had believed so, she didn't any more. How long had she been coming to the cemetery out of habit? Out of guilt? Whatever reasons she had now for the frequency of her visits, they no longer involved Henny.

Instead she went to Harriet's and leaned upon the stone. Benny bent to deadhead a marigold. Several more needed the same. Kneeling beside the little garden she had planted for this woman she'd never met but had known most of her life, she tucked the lily behind her ear and started pinching.

"I know you listen to me when I talk," she said. "Augie said you do, and now that I know he's not just me being nuts-o, I know you're here, too." She looked up at the stars. "I don't know where Augie is, but he's not here with me so maybe he's with you. Can you tell him I saw his kids' handprints?"

No squeeze. Not even a ruffle of breeze. But there never had been before. As always, Harriet wasn't talking.

"He broke up the patio," Benny told her anyway. "Dan did, I mean. But he couldn't bring himself to throw away those handprints. He said they belonged in the yard. He's such a mush." Benny chuckled. "Even when we were kids, he tried to be so cool, but he didn't fool anyone. I never understood why he didn't have girlfriends like Tim did. He was good-looking, still is. He wasn't the kind of guy who ogled the girls or made them feel trashy. And he's funny in a goofy way. There were rumors about his parents, like his dad smacked his mom around. I don't know if they're true or not, but…"

Benny sighed, and then she straightened, stretched her back. She wondered what time it was. It had to be getting late. She checked her cell phone. Ten 'til nine, and several missed calls from her mother. Fabulous. She pressed the call-back.

"Hey, Ma."

"Where are you?"

"I'm at the cemetery."

"At this hour?"

"I went over to Evelyn Taylor's place but the party was already over. I just stopped in here on my way home to finish up something I was doing earlier. I'm heading home now."

"Just be careful."

"I'm always careful. Don't worry, okay?"

"All right."

"Liar." Benny laughed softly. "I love you."

"I love you too, Benny. See you soon. I'll make tea."

Benny rose groaning to her feet.

"Good-night, Harriet," she said. "Tell Augie I will be back soon. Not tomorrow. I have a doctor appointment. Crap. I forgot to ask my brother about the car."

She texted Peter as she walked to her scooter.

Can i use yr car 2morrow

Just as she was tucking her cell into her pocket, it buzzed.

If i can use yr scoot

Kk thanx

She placed the lily onto her scooter seat, put her helmet on. If not for that fragrant, white flower, tea with her mother might, just might, help her forget the soft way Dan looked at her, and how it made her feel like there were bees in her shoes, in her hair, buzzing under her skin. She picked it up. She inhaled its scent, looked back toward Harriet's grave where she could leave it and not feel bad for doing so, then placed it carefully into her milk-crate basket, legged over the scooter, and headed for home.

* * * *

"She was waiting for you."

"I know, Harriet. I tried but it's exhausting."

"I wouldn't know."

"Maybe you should try it then."

"And maybe you should mind your own affairs, you miscreant, and leave mine to me."

"You are a puzzle, Harriet."

"Good. I aim to keep it such. A woman's got to maintain her mystery."

"Why, Harriet, are you flirting with me?"

"No. I leave the flirting to you, for what good it will do you. She's spoke for, you know."

"Her husband is—"

"Not him, you rattlebrain. The other man. The one she was talking about. Daniel."

"What makes you say this?"

"I got my reasons."

"Reasons you won't share with me?"

"Not my place to tell tales."

"But you started it."

"You jealous?"

"I...I think I am."

"Then you're daft, too."

"So are you going to tell me?"

"No."

"You are no fun, Harriet Gardner Farcus. No fun at all."

Chapter 7

Whip-poor-wills

Driving had never been her thing. Benny didn't get her license until she was nineteen, and only then because her mother insisted. She didn't like being encased in what was essentially a humungous bullet in need of a target. Her scooter limited her travels, but driving it was better than feeling like the itchy finger on a trigger.

She drove too slow, as evidenced by the horns honking and the other cars passing the moment the dotted line appeared in the road. White-knuckled and grumpy, Benny finally pulled into the clinic parking lot. She was ten minutes late even though she had given herself an extra half-hour to get there. Slamming the door made her feel slightly better. She walk-trotted across the steamy asphalt, up the steps, and into the ridiculously crowded but blissfully cool waiting room.

Benny signed in. At least a dozen names came before hers.

"How long do you think it will be?" she asked the unsmiling receptionist.

"An hour. Maybe a little more. Depends."

"But I had an appointment for eleven o'clock."

The receptionist glanced at her watch. "So did three other women here, and they were on time. Have a seat, Ms. Grady. I'll bring you a cup of tea in a few minutes."

Benny found a seat between two heavily pregnant women. Good as her word, the receptionist brought out a tray with not one but several steaming cups of what smelled like chamomile tea. Holding the cup in both hands, she inhaled the steam before sipping. Chamomile always reminded her of high school and autumn days sitting on the porch swing under the stairs with her mother. Their ritual, every day, this tea when she got home from school. Only through the coldest parts of winter did they take the ritual into the kitchen.

"Is this your first?" the woman to her left asked.

"Yes, it is. Yours?"

"Hell, no." She hooted. "My fourth. And my last."

"That's what you said with the last little one, Teresa," the woman on her right teased. "And the one before and the one before."

"You hush. That wriggler you got in there is your fourth, too."

"But I don't keep saying it's the last. I'll have as many babies as the Good Lord lets me."

"Good Lord, nothing, Colette. It's all to do with that man of yours. Never knew a man couldn't keep it in his pants like him."

"At least mine knows how to use his. Can't figure how you keep getting pregnant when we all know your man takes them blue pills to get his up."

Benny tried not to laugh as they got more and more vulgar, and failed. But they hurled obscene comments about their husbands' attributes and prowess with the good-natured feel of women who knew one another well, probably went way back. Several of the other waiting women were quick to join in. Benny envied their camaraderie. She'd only shared her pregnancy with Henny, and a woman dead a hundred years, both silent as the grave.

"So how far along are you?" Colette asked, and the room quieted. Waited.

"Only about four months. I'm here for my first ultrasound."

"You'll like that. Makes it real. Get them to print out a picture for you."

"I will." *Though I have no one to show it to.* The loneliness of it all hit Benny hard. She suddenly wished for her mother, for Savvy, for anyone she loved to be there with her to share the experience with.

Damn Henny. Damn Dan. It just wasn't supposed to be this way.

"What's wrong, girl?" Colette asked. "Why're you crying?"

"It's a very long and complicated story." Benny couldn't seem to stop herself. In this company of women, strangers and sisters at the same time, Benny spilled her guts in soft tears and gentle sobs amid crooning clucks from the other women gathered in closer. From Henny's death to Valentine's Day to the night prior in the dark garden with the oblivious father of her child, she told them everything—except about Augie. Him, she kept firmly to herself.

"That's a lot of drama, there," Teresa shook her head. "Good enough to be on TV."

"So that's what a white girl like you is doing at this place." Colette whistled. "I didn't figure on all that."

Benny startled. "There are other white women here besides me."

"Sure there are, but not like you. We're all here 'cause we're poor and have no health insurance worth a damn. I can tell you're not poor. You don't have the look."

Benny's glance flickered from face to face, then she blushed for doing so. She had never considered herself well off, but neither did she ever feel poor. Her parents had worked hard all their lives. They owned a home without a mortgage, always had food and fuel and a little something extra to pay for a vacation somewhere warm when winter lingered too long. She and Henny had been the same, living in safe poverty upstairs from her parents, where she still lived now on her survivor benefits, state-supplemented insurance, and the small but sufficient salary she made working at Savvy's. She even managed to save a bit in the yet-to-be-used travel fund.

These women had never been on vacation. They had no savings. They lived day to day, paycheck to paycheck. They went to the childbirth clinic where the wait time was always several hours even with an appointment because they had no other choice, not because they didn't want anyone in their town to know they were pregnant. Black women. White women. Asian and Latina women. Colette was right. Benny did not look like them. She couldn't put her finger on what it was setting her apart, but she felt it. Keenly. And it made her feel like crying all over again.

"Colette," the receptionist called. The woman beside her rose awkwardly to her feet.

"You got to tell that man he's having a baby," she said. "Make sure he pays you child support."

"You're a stone-cold fish, Colie." Teresa shook her head. "This has nothing to do with money. Isn't that right, Benny?"

"Colette? You coming or you want to give your spot to someone else?"

"I'm coming, Trudy. Hold your water. Lord knows, I can't." Then to Benny. "Just tell him."

"I will." Benny sniffed. "Thank you, Colette."

Teresa took her hand as Colette waddled away, patted it. "You're going to be just fine. You'll see."

Benny nodded. The sensation of being watched lingered a few moments longer, then faded. The room went silent again, except for the sound of magazine pages turning. But Teresa kept her hand gently in hers.

* * * *

It was nearly one o'clock before the receptionist, Trudy, called Benny's name. Colette and Teresa were already seen and gone, but not without giving Benny their phone numbers.

"You call," Colette said.

"Anytime," Teresa added.

And they had left together, despite all their arguing.

Benny sat on the exam table in a gown that wouldn't close over her boobs, a drape over her legs, and needing to pee. The door opened.

"Oh."

Benny nearly peed on the table. "Savvy. What? What are you...?"

"Doing here?" Savannah closed the door behind her and opened the file in her hand. "The same thing I do every Wednesday. I would ask you what you're doing here but I see by the chart it's a sixteen-week ultrasound. The tech will be in shortly. You haven't been in since your first appointment confirming your pregnancy. I'd like to do a quick exam, unless you have some objection."

"Objection. N—no. You're a doctor?"

"OB/GYN," Savannah answered. "Shimmy down to the end here and put your feet in the stirrups."

Benny did as she was told, mesmerized and astonished and close to spewing the kind of laughter that turned quickly to tears. "I'm not sure I'll be able to look you in the eye again."

"I've seen lots of cooches in my day, sugar. Yours is no different."

Savannah performed her exam quickly, gently. Benny gasped anyway.

"I see you drank the water you were told to."

"I admit, I peed about an hour ago." Benny squirmed. "I couldn't hold it anymore. But I did drink the tea Trudy brought me, and a bottle of water besides since then. I'm hurting just as bad now, so it's okay, right?"

"If you can hold it a squinch longer, yes. It makes the image a bit better. Our machine is an older one."

"I can. Sure. But just a squinch. I think I might die soon if I can't pee."

"Such drama." Savannah squeezed her foot. "I'll get the tech."

Benny lay on the table, staring at the ceiling. "This is surreal," she muttered. "What next? Is Dan going to walk in to fix a lightbulb?"

Savvy returned with a device that looked like an old transistor radio. "The tech's going to be a few minutes."

Benny came up on her elbows. "What's that thing?"

"Fetal heart Doppler. Haven't you heard your baby's heartbeat yet?"

Benny looked at the device, at Savannah, and shook her head.

"Well, lay back. It's time you did."

Savannah exposed Benny's belly, squeezed clear goop onto her skin. "Sorry, it's a little cold. There are warmers available, but we can't afford one. We usually have to wait for the hospital to donate old equipment when they get new." The Doppler clicked on, a static squeak that jolted through Benny. Savannah stretched out the coiled cord, slid the wand microphone around in the goop. Static bumps and swishy sounds crackled out of the speaker, and then…

Whoosh-swhoosh-whoosh-swhoosh.

Like a jump rope out of childhood, muffled by years and years. The steady sound of her baby's heartbeat sent waves of joy skating over Benny's skin.

"Amazing, isn't it?" Savannah whispered. "The size of a banana, and already making so much noise."

The door opened and in sailed a woman who could not have topped five feet with heels on. Savannah moved back, and the jump rope sound vanished. "She's already gooped."

The tech stepped onto the stepstool beside the ultrasound machine and gooped her up again anyway.

After the initial gasp, Benny relaxed. The tiny being growing inside her wriggled and jumped like a cricket on the grainy screen.

"There is the spine." Savannah pointed while the tech took measurements. "And ribs. A femur right there. Can you see it, Benny?"

"Yes," she whispered. The clear outline of brow, nose, lips, chin filled her up. Love was not a strong enough word, but there were no others that came as close. Tears rolled down the side of her face. Benny wiped them quickly away, wishing.

"Do you want to know the sex?" the tech asked.

"Can you tell already?"

"If the little one cooperates. Sure."

"Okay, yes. But it's a boy," Benny said. "I know it is."

The three watched the screen in silence as the tech's wand glided all over Benny's belly and suddenly stopped.

"Do you see, Doctor?"

"I do. Couldn't ask for a better view."

"What?" Benny asked. "I don't know what I'm looking at."

Savvy and the tech laughed. "You're looking at your little girl's lady-bits," Savvy told her. "Sorry, sugar. It's not a boy."

Benny squinted at the screen. "You sure?"

"There is never one hundred percent with this old machine," the tech said. "But I would give it a ninety-eight point five percent you've got a baby girl cooking. You want a picture?"

"Yes, please."

The tech click-click-clicked and a grainy image curled out of the printer. She handed it to Benny. "Baby's first photo-shoot." Then to Savannah, "I'll put the results in her file, but everything looks good. The baby measures right for sixteen weeks." The tech waved and left.

Savannah flipped through Benny's file as if she were really reading it. "Savvy?"

Savannah stilled. When she looked up, her eyes were bright. "There was no reason to tell you or anyone what I was in Georgia, and what I do here. I volunteer my time at this clinic. It's not my job. My job is the farm."

"You don't have to explain anything," Benny assured her. "I was just going to say I'll keep your secret if you keep mine. Well, I'd keep it anyway, but you know what I mean."

"It's not a secret," Savannah said. "I just don't broadcast it. And you, my friend, are not going to be able to keep—oh."

"Oh?"

"Your trip to North Carolina. This is why you're going, not to get away from Bitterly."

Benny averted her gaze. "I do need to get away, and the reasons are still valid."

"No they are not, Benedetta. The trip went from something you needed to do to running away."

"I just want to figure things out before the shit hits the fan."

"What is there to figure out? You're stalling."

"And? Is that so bad?"

"Benny." Savannah sat next to her on the exam table. "I can't even imagine what you've got going through that pretty head of yours, but I know you well enough by now to get you."

"Get me?"

"Yes, get you. You're an avoider. Avoiders only move forward by accident. You are never going to get over Henny's death if you continue to avoid life, but that's your choice. There is no choice where this baby is concerned. Avoid facing it all you like. In the end, she is going to arrive whether you want her to or not."

"I want her to. It's not like I don't want her too. Yeesh. I want her so bad. I'm already madly in love with her, and until a few minutes ago, I thought she was a boy. It's just…" Benny put her head in her hands. "…complicated."

Savannah put her arms around her. "It doesn't have to be."

Benny leaned into her friend…boss…doctor. Phantom or real, she smelled the farm on Savannah's skin. Rich earth. Flowers. Sunshine and rain. This woman who claimed life need not be so complicated had left behind her home, whatever family remained there, and a medical career she kept hidden, if not secret.

Those who live in glass houses…

Benny quelled the unkind thought and lifted her head. "You planning on asking me who the father is?"

"That wouldn't be my place, as a doctor." Savvy smiled. "But I have a pretty good idea. He is the only man you've been out with in all the years I've known you."

"How do you know?"

"Bitterly is a small town, sugar. He's a good man. He cares for you. And I believe you care for him."

"But I can't."

"Yes. You can." Savannah kissed her cheek. "Now scoot. I have a lot more patients to see before I can go home tonight."

Benny hopped off the table, clutching closed the too-small gown. "You won't tell him, will you?"

"Of course not."

"Thanks, Savvy. I will. I promise. In my time, okay?"

"All right." Savannah started from the room. "Just remember you didn't make your baby alone. If you won't let him into your life, for your daughter's sake, let him into hers."

Chapter 8

Summon Twilight To The Trees

The drive home went better. No one beeped, or passed her. Not that she would have noticed, anyway. Benny's thoughts flickered in and about her head like the lightning bugs on the arbor in Dan's back yard. Savannah was right. Dan was a good man who deserved all the joy she was keeping from him. And he cared for her. Benny could no more deny it than the fact that she cared for him too, maybe even loved him, if only Henny's ghost didn't haunt her so.

It's not me. It's you. I'm sorry, Benny.

Tears welled. She wiped them quickly, quelled them completely. She thought instead about Savannah, and what might have happened to pull her out of the south, away from all she had ever known, and a medical career she had to have worked hard for.

Everyone, she had said when Benny asked who she'd lost. How tempting it had been to leave the childbirth clinic and sit in the car, searching the internet for clues to her friend's past, but she didn't. If Savannah wanted to share that with her, she'd have done so by now.

Curiosity and conjecture carried her home with no more tears. It was mid-afternoon by the time she drove through town and spotted her scooter parked outside the coffeehouse. She parked and got out of her car. Peter wasn't in there. She moved on to CC's and found him leaning on the counter, talking to a tall redhead she barely recognized for the masses of silky red hair draped over her shoulder.

"Charlotte?"

"Benny!" The younger woman threw her arms in the air and scurried around the counter to pull Benny into a tight hug. "How are you?"

"I'm fine, thanks. What are you doing here?"

"I came up for the weekend to get Caleb. He's going to spend a couple weeks with me down in Cape May."

"Ah, so you talked him into it."

"What did he say? He doesn't want to come?"

"No, just that he didn't want to spend the whole summer."

"Whew!" Charlotte wiped the back of her hand dramatically across her brow. "He'll have a blast. It's great down there."

"I've never been."

"You should come. I've almost convinced your brother to visit."

Benny looked to Peter, who blushed but winked. "She bribed me with cookies."

Charlotte smacked his arm. "Nice. And here I thought it was my sparkling personality luring you."

"That too, but what pushed it over the edge was the cookies. Pay up."

"You're coming, then?"

"I'll let you know after I get the cookies."

Charlotte clapped her hands, scurried around the counter, and started putting cookies in a box.

Benny bit the insides of her cheeks to keep the smirk from her face.

Peter had always been a notorious flirt. His blue eyes and dimples made it way too easy. But Charlotte McCallan, with her then-pixie-cut hair and Seattle-grunge fashion sense, had never been so bubbling-over enthusiastic. More had changed in the few years she spent in culinary school and Cape May than the length of her hair.

"Want your car back?" Benny jingled the keys. "I'm going out to the farm, and then the cemetery before heading home."

"Sure, thanks." Peter took the keys, handed Benny hers. "You want me to put your bags in your apartment?"

"Bags?"

"Didn't you go shopping up in Lee?"

Benny wasn't clueless enough to hope he was equally so. "Yeah, well, I didn't go shopping. I had a doctor appointment and didn't want to tell Ma."

"Anything serious?"

Benny pursed her lips. "No, not serious. Girly stuff, dude. You don't want to know."

"Oh." Now he blushed. "Gotcha."

"Thanks for letting me use the car."

"No problem."

"Before I hand these over"—Charlotte held the box of cookies just out of Peter's reach—"I want a solemn promise from you that you are coming to visit me this summer."

"I'll go you one better." Peter leaned on the counter, dimples deepening. "How about I come down for a long weekend when it's time for Caleb to go home. I'll save you the trip north."

"Deal." Charlotte handed Peter the box and hugged him at the same time. "This is great. Oh! You'll be down for the Fourth of July. Fireworks on the beach. You'll love it."

"I'm going to head out," Benny said before Charlotte launched into all the ways Cape May was amazing. "Thanks again, Peter. See you, Charlotte."

"See you, Benny."

Benny legged over her scooter and strapped on the helmet she had insisted Peter wear. It was too big, and still brand new even though it was seven years bought in June.

Checking in at the farm, she found all running smoothly without her and Savannah. Though most of those working were high school students, Edgardo and Raul had been farming all their lives. Though they were her foremen, Savannah called them her mentors, which always made them smile proudly, nod their heads and wave her off. Benny suspected they spoke little English, but they knew the land and how to treat it with respect. From it, they grew the best vegetables Bitterly had ever eagerly consumed.

From the farm, she went to the cemetery, and only once did she think about her baby girl, and only half-a-thought went to Dan. She would take them both out later. Instead she focused on Augie and the hand-prints she had seen with her own eyes. Now that she knew she wasn't nuts-o, she had a few questions for him.

* * * *

"Turn it off! Turn it off!"

Dan closed the water-main valve behind the caretaker's cottage in Bitterly Cemetery. Water sprayed up at him, leaking out yet another crack in the piping. By the time he got it shut, he was drenched.

And so was Charlie. Palming off the water streaming down his face, Charlie squished over to the broken valve. "That too, huh?"

"What makes you think that? Looks perfectly sound to me."

"Funny, Dan. Real funny." Charlie let go a deep breath. "This whole system needs replacing. I just don't have the time."

"It's a tough thing to come by, these days," Dan agreed. "I'm busier than I like to be myself. No time to fart let alone fish."

"Blasphemy."

The men laughed together, in the way of old friends making jokes made a hundred times before.

"I'd put in a work order," Charlie said, "but by the time the town officials approve it we'll both be old men."

"Or dead. What are you doing Friday?"

"Fixing the sprinkler system, I suppose."

"Funny how that works." Dan grinned. "I am too. We can divert this damaged area with a garden hose for now. Won't work in the long term, but it'll get the lawns watered a couple days."

"If we divert here, we don't have the timers."

"Then I suppose one of us is going to have to come and turn them on, and the other's got to turn them off."

"Which do you want?" Charlie asked. "On at seven or off at nine?"

"I'll turn them off. I'm closer to town."

"You sure you don't mind coming out again?"

"What else have I got to do?"

Charlie only raised an eyebrow.

"I walked right into that one. I been telling you since she dumped my ass last winter, leave it be, Charlie."

"Benny's worth fighting for."

"Of course she is," Dan grumbled. "But she doesn't want—"

"You don't know that. You're assuming. She came to the party, didn't she? Long after it was over. Why do you think she did that?"

"Not to see me."

"You're an idiot."

"Never claimed otherwise."

"Daniel." Charlie shook his wet, shaggy head. "We've been friends since before we were born. I never saw you as happy as you were that week with Benny."

"So?"

"So?" Charlie shoved his shoulder. "Don't you want to be happy?"

"I been miserable so long, I don't think I know how to be anything else."

"That's not funny."

"Wasn't meant to be."

"Dan, come on. Just think, where would I be if I gave up on Johanna?"

"Not all of us have your stamina. Twenty years is a long time to wait for a woman."

"If you give up on Benny, what are you going to be in twenty years besides sixty and lonely?"

"And if I keep trying, I'll be sixty, lonely, and a failure."

Charlie clapped him on the back, his smile spreading instead of fading. "Giving up is the only failure. You know that better than most. Now help me get the hose hooked up before I give in to my more primitive instincts to whack some sense into your stubborn skull."

"Like to see you try," Dan called after him. Charlie only waved over his shoulder. There was a time Tim would have made good on the threat. Henny would have too. But Charlie? He was no more likely to take a whack at him than Dan would do the same. They were the peacekeepers, the ones who stepped in when hotter tempers flared. Dan even remembered, like water splashed in his face, consoling Benny after an argument with her then-boyfriend, when they were all just kids and she and Henny still had a dozen years to kiss and make up. He had no memory of what the fight had been about, or why he ended up with her in his arms. Dan did remember the feel of her breath on his neck, of her tears seeping into the fabric of his shirt, and how angry he was with Henny for making her cry.

Dan grimaced. Memory made way for memory. The young woman weeping in his arms became the same woman resting her head to his chest just to listen to the beat of his heart. Benny, who smelled like flowers, whose skin was silk against his rough hands, who vanished in the night like a dream he couldn't call back no matter how bad he wanted to.

Chapter 9

Among The Hollows

"I told you she would come, Harriet. Didn't I tell you?"
"She said she wasn't."
"She can't stay away from me. I have that effect on women."
"Oh, so you remember that now."
"I remember more than I used to."
"That's the bad part, August. Remembering things best left to lie."
"Stop being a defeatist. Do you remember all I told you?"
"I'm not the one with the memory problem."
"Good. Then be ready. And no making up tales to make me look bad."
"I won't have to, you delinquent. You're bad enough to start."

* * * *

Benny went straight to Augie's grave. Before she took off her helmet, the faint whispering not heard by her ears, but someplace inside her head, began. She dropped to the ground, sitting cross-legged, and listened.

"I know you're there," she said. "But I'm having a hard time understanding you."

A sensation like fingers tickling up her back straightened her spine from its slouch.

"Oh! Don't do that. Okay, I get it. You're behind me. I won't look."

Those fingers squeezed her shoulder.

"Is something wrong, Augie? Why can't you talk to me like always?"

Nothing happened for a long stretch of moments.

Benny closed her eyes while she waited, reclined in the grass, arms behind her head. To keep her thoughts from wandering to those places she was trying to avoid, she filled her head with birdsong and breezes, with the occasional swish of a car passing on the road below Bitterly Cemetery, with sunlit warmth on her skin. Benny thought about going to get her sunscreen, but she'd left her purse in Peter's car.

"Is this better?"

Benny smiled. "Yes. But it's faint, and I can't hear you so much as feel the words inside my head. You must be in deeper water."

Augie laughed, the sound like skittering leaves and not the one that made her want to join in.

"Deeper, yes. Benedetta?"

"What is it, Augie? You seem...nervous."

"It is because I have a confession to make."

"All right. Out with it."

"It is time to tell you my true reason for seeking you out, *cara mia*."

"Sounds ominous," Benny teased. "You're not going to do some kind of bodysnatching thing on me, are you?"

"I would make a wicked response but Harriet would not like it, and I am counting on her help."

"Harriet is with us?"

"Harriet is always lurking about. She's been haunting this place a long time."

"How will she help?"

Augie was silent a moment. "When I am in that deep place, where Harriet waits, I remember things I forget again when I am closer to life. I told Harriet everything I wish to say. She will tell me, and then I will repeat it to you."

"Like telephone."

"Yes. You and Harriet are the receivers. I am the operator between. All in different depths."

"I meant the game...never mind." Benny sat cross-legged on his grave. Goosebumps prickled. Excited. Nervous. Maybe even scared? She always believed life and death were not so far apart, but Benny had never imagined how close, in fact, they were. "Go ahead. I'm listening."

* * * *

"You must remain silent, Benedetta, and do not ask questions no matter how much you might want to. It is a difficult thing I do, like holding open two doors but my arms are only just long enough to reach.

"I believe I am bound here, barred from moving beyond this place, because I made a promise I did not keep, to my little daughter, Flora.

"Flora? Are you certain? My daughter's name was...oh. Yes, I remember her now. You were right, Harriet. Remembering is painful. Ah, Flora was so small when I left Italy for America. She wore her hair in pigtails, tied up with ribbons.

"Yes, Harriet. I do need you. Sorry, sorry. Go ahead.

"I left Italy in 1928, a year before the Crash. I came to America to find employment and earn money to send for my wife and child. This was the promise I made, that I would bring her to America and we would be together again. Leaving Flora broke my heart, but I was happier to leave Carmen than I was sad to leave my child. My wife and I, our marriage was arranged. We did not like one another much. She used to wait for me to come home from work, wooden spoon in hand and—"

"No, Harriet. Don't go. I will save my remembering for another time. I know this is exhausting work and—yes, yes, I will shut my mouth. Please, continue."

Benny shifted on her bottom, rubbed at the shivers still making all the hair on her body stand on end.

"The Stock Market crashed," Augie said, his voice a little stronger. "There was no work. I had to choose whether to stay in America and hope for better times, or go back to Italy where everything was so much worse. I stayed. I sent money home when I could. Now and then, I would get a letter from my Flora, never from Carmen, my wife. Years passed. Three, I think. But for Christmas greetings and birthdays, the letters had stopped coming. Until I got a letter from my wife saying she married another man. She told our daughter I died. She told everyone, even my mother. My poor mama. It was a terrible thing to do, and worse, I went along with it.

"Are you certain, Harriet? This is what I told you? Or did you add it in yourself? Yes, I thought so. Very well, you're right. It was a terrible thing I did. I am paying for it now, no? Continue, please.

"I was young. I thought my child better off without me, or chose to believe so. I married again and settled here in Bitterly. I had a good life. A happy life. I didn't forget my first child, but I did keep her secret. My Katherine never knew I had been married, or had a child before any of ours. I wish there had been a deep bond between Flora and me. Alas, she was a girl, and her mother kept her close. Strange, no? I should remember this now?

"Fine, Harriet. For all your snipping and snapping at me, I would think you'd be happy for the pain of these memories, to know you were right about—okay. Okay. Yes, you are old. You are cranky too. Continue. I promise I will not drift off again."

Difficult as it was, Benny managed not to laugh, or ask questions when it seemed to take forever for him to speak again.

"I lost all connection to Flora. For a long time, I knew nothing of her life, if she grew to be a woman, or even survived the war. I thought about her less and less. I was no longer Augusto, but August. Life before coming to America was erased.

"Beyond the grave, all my wrongs came back at me. It is a consequence of death, this review of one's life. I broke my mother's heart, but sons are ever doing such things. I had three brothers, all who thought me dead. The only one who knew differently kept her secret, for her wrongs were as deep as mine. But my daughter, the child of my own blood, I abandoned her to whatever fate Carmen's choice gave her. I did not return for her. I let her grieve a daughter's grief. And this is now my grief, so deep I am stuck here until I can somehow make it right.

"Harriet believes I am keeping myself bound, as a sort of penance. But I was never so noble a man, and even if, by some chance, I am, the result is the same. I need to find my daughter. I can no longer keep my promise to make us a family. But perhaps I can give her the brothers and sister she should have had. I want her to know I loved her, and I am sorry for the choices I made. Maybe she will not forgive me, and if she can't I will stay forever bound. But maybe she will, and then I can let go of this world and journey to whatever comes next."

* * * *

"Oh, Augie," Benny says, eyes still closed. "You abandoned your wife and little girl."

"Like I abandoned you." It is Henny's voice, not Augie's. Benny sits up. Where is Augie's grave? The wood beyond? There is only a headstone with a name too familiar, and pansies, impatiens, and marigolds as far as she can see. Henny is there, a man in his twenties.

"You didn't abandon me, love," Benny tells him. "You died."

"Amounts to the same thing, doesn't it? I'm here. You're alone. Not so different from your friend."

"He made a choice. You didn't."

"Didn't I?" He picks a flower from the grave-garden she planted for him, smells it and smiles. "I've never been here."

"Here? Your grave?"

He nods.

"How is that so?"

"I don't know," he tells her. "Just never have been. It's nice."

"Henny?" Benny looks behind him, glances over her shoulder. "Is there anyone else here?"

"Just me and you, baby. This is our place."

"But I'm here all the time and I never—"

"Not the cemetery." Henny laughs and Benny feels it in the pit of her stomach. "This is your doing, not mine. You brought it with you. I'm talking about this place, Ben, where you and I will always be together."

He pushes off the tombstone, holds out a hand for hers. Benny lets him pull her up and Henny holds her gently. No skin-on-skin, but there is contact of a different kind, like Augie's voice when it is felt, not heard.

"I will never leave you," Henny says, tracing the forget-me-not tattooed on her wrist. "I will always be here, when you need me."

"Be where?" Benny pulls away. "I don't under—"

"You do." He touches her nose with a kiss that feels like sunshine. "You've been finding me here all along."

"I don't want to have to find you. I want you by my side."

Henny's smile fades. He steps back, holds out his hand. "Then walk with me," he tells her. "Take my hand, and walk with me."

Benny reaches. Her fingers tremble. Her hand falls to her side again. Henny smiles the smile she knows so well, the one she alternately wanted to kiss and smack. All-knowing. Cocky. Confident. And gone. He is waving from the cemetery road, from the place she parks her scooter. He legs over, kicks it to roaring life. No hairdryer engine, but more powerful. And now it is not a scooter, but the motorcycle he died on.

"See you." He waves, revs the engine, and glides away.

She watches him go, her hand moving to her belly and the fluttering there. Always fluttering. A little jumping cricket whose song is the whoosh-swoosh *of a jump-rope when Benny was a little girl.*

* * * *

"Benny? Hey, you okay?"

Blinking, gaining her bearings, Benny came up on her elbows. Charlie McCallan stood over her blocking the sunlight. Her mouth tasted like she'd guzzled sour milk, her muscles were stiff. She sat up. On Augie's grave.

"I'm…fine. I guess…I fell asleep."

"Guess you did."

No Augie. No Henny. Benny spotted her scooter on the narrow cemetery road, Charlie's truck parked behind it. Further down the road, a sky-blue minivan. Otherwise, not a soul. None that she could actually see, anyway. Or sense. She held out her hands.

"Give me a hand, will you?"

Charlie helped her to her feet, holding her steady while her cramped muscles loosened. "What are you doing at this end of the cemetery, anyway?"

Benny brushed herself off, pretended he hadn't asked a question and instead asked one of her own. "How'd you get so wet?"

"Water valve burst."

"Sounds like fun." She laughed. "It's getting late. I'd better get home."

Charlie watched her out of the corner of his eye, but he made no more comment about where she'd been sleeping. Dreaming. Communing with the dead. Whatever it was Benny had been doing, it left her exhausted, and she wondered if it was the same kind of soul-weariness Augie and Harriet experienced. She thanked Charlie, promised she'd come by soon to see renovations he made to the old farmhouse on County Line Road, and started up her scooter thankfully still there and not turned into a motorcycle and gone.

Chapter 10

Firefly-seeds

The habit of always having a change of clothes on hand, a lesson learned as a boy always staining, tearing or otherwise destroying them, never left him. Getting the back of his father's hand hadn't been enough to teach him, but his mother's tears while she scrubbed or mended were.

The first time Daniel Greene the elder smacked his wife for not raising a more conscientious son, Dan Greene the younger learned to leave a spare set tied up tight in a garbage bag, hidden in the hollow of a tree in the woods behind his house. When he ruined too many pairs of jeans to go unnoticed, he started changing into the already-ruined stuff before going off with his friends. No one said anything about his ragged clothes. Henny. Tim. Charlie. They knew enough not to.

Dan shoved the wet stuff into his duffle bag, tossed it into the back seat of the minivan. His sister's car was, in his opinion, the most hideous thing he'd ever seen on four wheels. Sky blue. Rusted out wheel wells. Cracks and tears in the upholstery, and carpeting stinking like unwashed gym socks. She sold her Land Rover after Paul left, and bought the cheapest thing still running. When Mabel cried earlier that morning, mortified for her mother to pick up her friends in the blue beast, Dan had given his sister the keys to his pickup and told her to make sure the kids didn't eat in it.

"I just had it detailed," he'd grumbled. Evelyn had kissed his cheek. Mabel hugged him around the waist. Joss didn't seem to notice, his eyes being glued to the game he was playing on his mother's cell phone.

Dan rolled down all the windows, one at a time, and got into the driver's seat. It took a couple tries, but the van started up. The car was pointed in the wrong direction to take the quick, if illegal, way out. The cemetery road was a one-way, something Dan always found amusing.

It was late. Few ever visited. Still, he followed the rules and drove the whole circuit through.

Well-spaced trees dotted tranquil, rolling lawns. Weller Woods hugged the whole west end, the oldest part of the cemetery. Most of the earliest settlers were laid to rest in that shaded sanctuary up against the wood. The Bossy family, the Wellers—they had whole sections reserved for them and their descendants, but they were not the oldest residents of Bitterly Cemetery. Many of those had no markers, having been buried on family land before there was a cemetery. Only one was marked, as far as Dan knew, and he did only because his best friend was buried beside her.

The car rolled to a stop where the sun still shined down on a wide expanse of lawn looking a little parched for the heat and broken sprinkler system. Dan let it idle. A discreet metal marker read: Rolling Green 183. The familiar debate ruffled through his head, to the same outcome. He switched off the ignition. He got out of the car. Three rows back, he found her.

Miranda Irene Greene
April 16, 1952 ~ July 7, 1993

"Hi, Mom."

He said no more. Never felt the need. Dan simply bowed his head and remembered her smile, the touch of her hand, the way her hair curved under her chin in a perfect, platinum wave. He conjured her peaches-and-cream skin and the pale green eyes she shared with him. Whenever the bruising bloomed in these memories, Dan forced it back. He wouldn't remember her as his father's victim. She deserved better, even if she never believed so herself.

The sound of a car rolling slowly by turned his head. Dan returned Charlie's wave, could not help smiling as the truck wound away. Their fearsome foursome got whacked in half when Henny died and Tim moved away, but if he had to choose which of them he'd stick close with, it was Charlie.

As he turned away from his mother's grave, he noticed Charlie's brake lights brighten. He slowed, stopped, and only then did Dan see Benny's scooter in the shaded part of the cemetery where all the best families took up space. He hurried to the van where he could spy on her from its safe anonymity. Charlie and Benny talked. He helped her to rise. A moment later, she was zipping beyond the shady wood and out of sight. Charlie's truck remained visible only a moment longer. Dan started the van and drove slowly, stopping where he thought she'd been parked.

What was Benny doing at this end of the cemetery? When they were kids, she used to hang out in the woods with her friends, but she wasn't a kid anymore. Her friends were grown or gone and no longer frequenting such places. Dan left the car idling, and got out. He picked his way among the tombstones, looking for some sign or reason for her to be there. Why in the heck did he care anyway? Dan chuckled to himself. When it came to Benedetta Marie Grady, there was no sense in his head. Nothing more to it than that.

All the headstones were Wellers, dating back to the 1800s when Bitterly became incorporated as a town. Dan knew little of the history, but he did know the Bossy and Weller families were the rich folk of their day. They owned the general store, the lumberyard, and any other business that served to put Bitterly on any map. They built the best houses, kept the best land, and often served on what sparse government existed in so small a town. There were stories, rumors, even a few scandals involving the families. Dan had no patience for gossip. As far as he was concerned, most, if not all of town history was a load of gossip made bigger by long winters and bored denizens. But one could not live in Bitterly without knowing the names on the tombstones he searched now for the one Benny had been visiting.

Back along the wrought-iron fence were the newer graves. There hadn't been a Weller descendant in Bitterly since 1976, and he only knew that because his sister and her then-husband bought the house from a family member long-gone from Bitterly, back in the mid-nineties. The family held onto the house for whatever reasons they had, but in the end, none of the Wellers wished to return to the town their family founded. The house was in bad shape, but Paul did right by it, Dan had to give him that. It was under his supervision the place was restored to what it had once been, right down to every odd quirk of the original builder.

Dan noticed the grass a bit flattened on one of those newer graves, wove his way to the site itself. The ground was definitely disturbed, as if someone had reclined in the grass. No wrappers or flowers or anything else to mark Benny's presence in evidence, Dan was nonetheless certain this was the right spot when he read the names on the tombstone.

Katherine Weller Fiore
September 13, 1919 ~ January 28, 1976
*

August Fiore
July 4, 1908 ~ July 7, 1980

The cold, slithery feeling started at the base of Dan's neck, worked up his scalp. She had blurted the name, pulled out the lie to toss at him, to get him to back off. He'd known it from the start, even if it didn't hurt any less. But there was a reason she'd picked the name, and Dan was looking at it.

Dan went back to the minivan and put it into drive, but he kept his foot on the brake. He rested his head to the steering wheel. "You were wrong, Charlie," he whispered. "Dead wrong."

Letting go a long exhale, he let up on the brake and rolled away. Benny hadn't come looking for him the night of Mabel's party. She came for the same reason she had been visiting this old-not-ancient grave.

Were there handprints in the concrete?

Why had she wanted to know? Bits fell into place. August Fiore built the house Dan lived in with his sister and her kids. His was the name Benny gave as her pretend-boyfriend. Benny had fallen asleep on his grave. No matter how he rearranged the bits, they simply did not form any kind of picture Dan could decipher. Something about this grave and those handprints meant something to her, and he was going to figure out what.

Daniel Greene played the fool, but he wasn't one. Charlie might have been wrong about the reason she showed up at a party already over, but Dan hadn't imagined her laughter, her smile, or the easy silence between them.

Chapter 11

The Cricket Knows Her

Benny's hands didn't shake putting the key into the lock, even if her insides felt like Jell-O. She entered her apartment and went straight to the couch flopping into it and closing her eyes. What was real? What was dreaming? And how much of either was her own brain insinuating itself into both?

What would have happened if she'd taken Henny's hand and followed where he led? Would Charlie have found her dead on Augie's grave? Or her husband's? The thought shuddered through her. Until Henny-in-her-dream held out his hand for hers, she hadn't realized just how much she didn't want to follow him into death, and it hurt almost as much as him dying in the first place.

Tears stung. Benny let them fall. She tried to tell herself it was because there were no guarantees that she would find her way to Henny. Augie's wife wasn't there to greet him when he died, after all. The lie tasted like metal in her mouth. The painful, glorious truth was Benny wanted to live.

She wanted to see her little cricket grow up, become a woman, and leave her. She wanted to love someone and be loved in return so the event was bittersweet and full of pride, not the end of meaning in her life. Those were the things she had wanted with Henny, things no longer possible. With him. But Benny had to admit, at last, she still wanted them.

Arms over her eyes, she stifled her sobs. The last thing she needed was her mother to come running. In her state, she would spill it all and that wasn't something Benny wanted to do just yet. She tried to think about Savannah, about Augie or Harriet or anything besides this simple, sincere wish to not only live, but to live happily, and couldn't. Shoving a throw pillow over her face, she screamed into it.

An arm slipped across her shoulders. Benny dropped the pillow. Nearly jumped out of the couch. Something fluttered up as if tossed, and to the ground. Peter pulled back, but his concerned eyes stayed on her.

"Sorry."

"You scared the crap out of me."

"You okay?"

"No."

"Want to talk about it?"

"No."

Peter picked up the square bit of paper. He placed it gently onto her lap. "You sure?"

Benny looked down at the ultrasound picture, her cricket floating oblivious, her bits and parts decipherable only because Savannah had pointed them out to her. Peter nudged her.

"Girly stuff?"

Her eyes shifted to him. "Peter, I…"

"You left it in my car," he said. "I wasn't snooping or anything."

"I didn't say you were." She picked up the picture, smiled a watery smile. "It's a girl."

Peter put his arm across her shoulder. "Do I have to ask who her father is?"

"Probably not." Benny nestled into his shoulder. "It was just the one time. One time in six years, and I get pregnant."

"You sorry?"

"No!"

"Then why are you being so secretive? It happens, Benny. It's not like you have to marry him or anything."

"I know. But…"

"But?"

"I might be kind of in love with him."

"Benny." Peter shifted, took her shoulders in both hands and shook her gently. "What the hell is wrong with you?"

"I know," she wailed. "That's why I haven't told anyone. Why I'm afraid to."

Peter quirked an eyebrow. "Not sure I follow you."

"Henny. My husband? How can I possibly love Dan Greene? I'm a fraud and an oath-breaker."

"Oath-breaker? You really are a dork."

"Shut up, Peter."

"You're also an idiot."

"Why am I an idiot?"

"Because that's not what I was getting at. Jeez, Ben. Henny's been gone for six years. Can you possibly believe this is what he wants? You never loving anyone? Ever?"

Benny grimaced. "It's what I promised him. Forever."

"And?"

"And falling in love with someone else breaks my promise."

Peter chuffed. "Does not."

"How do you figure that?"

"Did Ma and Dad stop loving Tim when you were born? Or you guys less when I was?"

"That's different. We're their children."

"It's not different." Peter took her hands, kissed one, then the other. "You were always my best playpal, Ben. I still get that all-lit up feeling inside when I see you. Call it a Pavlovian response of childhood. So when I say this, please know it's with all the love in my heart, okay?"

She sniffed. Nodded.

"You're dumb as a box of rocks."

"A dork, an idiot, and now dumb as a box of rocks. Gee, thanks."

Peter laughed and hugged her roughly. "Because you know love doesn't just go away. You, more than most people, are aware that a heart isn't a finite space. You're always going to love Henny, but it doesn't mean you can't love someone else, too."

"Doesn't it?" She hiccupped. "I'm afraid to find out."

Peter slumped back into the couch. "What are you going to do about Dan?"

"I'll tell him."

"When?"

"Soon."

"Before you go to North Carolina, or after?"

She gasped. "How did you...Tim."

"Of course, Tim. He called and asked if you were all right. Thank goodness I answered and not Ma."

The walls she built around her secret were crumbling, and with them went the ones she had unwittingly erected around her life. Benny pressed her hands to her cheeks.

"You won't tell, will you?"

"It's not for me to tell anyone anything," Peter answered. "Just don't be afraid to come to me, okay?"

Benny nodded. She let her hands fall. "When did you grow up, huh?"

"I'm not quite there yet." He said. "I love you, Ben. I can't stand seeing you cry."

"I'm kind of tired of crying myself."

They sat together in silence. Peter's love and concern prickled like clicks of static electricity flicking up and down her arms. When he was a baby, and she, nearly a teen, he had been her favorite plaything. Tim had no use for the squalling, often stinky bundle of baby boy, but Benny fell completely in love. Peter was her shadow, one she never tired of trailing alongside her. On the day she married Henny, he was twelve and completely enthralled by his brother-in-law. When Henny died, Peter had been all of twenty and still enthralled with the brother-in-law suddenly gone from his life.

"Oh." She sniffled. "Peter, I'm sorry."

"For?"

"Being so selfish. Grief does that, I guess. It narrows your vision down to a little pinprick that only lets you focus on yourself. But you lost him too. We all did."

"Yeah. You know what the worst part is, though?"

She shook her head.

"Seeing your light go out, Ben. You were always, I don't know, a free spirit. Always smiling. Laughing. Now, all you do is cry."

"I know." Benny rested a hand to her belly. The instant joy edged out the lingering sorrow. They were only flickers, but happiness was trying hard to flare back to life. "But things are changing, I think. I've got a better reason to stop letting grief being my whole world."

Peter rested his hand atop hers. "You are reason enough."

Her nose tickled. Her eyes stung. But Benny smiled a watery smile. Blowing her nose, she nudged him with her knee. "So? What's going on with Charlotte McCallan?"

Groaning, Peter flopped back into the couch. "We're just friends."

"You were flirting with her."

"I flirt with everyone."

"No interest, then? She's awfully pretty, and smart, and fun to be around."

"She also talks. A lot."

"True. You really going down to Cape May?"

"She gave me the cookies." He laughed. "It'll be fun. I have to get out of this town every once in a while."

"I'm surprised you haven't bolted yet. I always thought you'd be the one to fly, not Tim."

"I did too."

"So why haven't you—"

"Got any names picked out yet?"

They didn't speak quite at the same time. Benny was close to certain he'd cut her off. She let it go. Reluctantly. "Until today, I thought Cricket was a boy."

"Cricket?"

"That's what I've been calling her since I saw her jumping around on the screen. I have no idea what to name her."

"Cricket is kind of cute."

"If you're a celebrity who smokes a little too much weed, sure." She grimaced. "You have any other ideas?"

"Clarice?"

"After Ma?" Benny crinkled her nose. "No offense, but I'll pass. She's going to smother this baby girl enough as it is. Last thing I need is Ma making them matching outfits or something."

"Well, you'll think of something." He sat forward, propping himself with an elbow. "And maybe Dan will have an idea or two of his own."

"Let's not go back that way again, okay?"

"Okay." He pushed out of the couch and, simple as that, the subject dropped. "You want dinner? Ma put a plate aside for you."

"What did she make?"

"Chicken cutlets, a salad and corn on the cob. And biscuits."

"Hers?"

"Yup."

"Yum. Sounds like I want dinner."

Peter bent and kissed her cheek. Benny closed her eyes and let the joy of talking to him bloom. How long had it been since she allowed these little bursts of joy? She'd felt it, certainly, but curtailed it as quickly as it came. Like Valentine's Day, when she woke to the stars and the cold and Dan's body keeping her warm as a gooey marshmallow, when the joy burst so bright she would weep, only to remember Henny and grief and leave Dan where he slept.

Stop, Benny. Now.

"I'll be down in a few." She rose from the couch, adjusting the jeans riding up on her. She had to go shopping, buy some hippie-dresses she'd be more comfortable in. Dresses that would let her hide just a little longer. "I'm going to wash up a bit."

In the bathroom, splashing water on her face, Benny looked closely at her face in the mirror. She looked the same as she did ten years ago, in her estimation. Her skin was still soft, unlined, and unblemished. She

had never believed herself extraordinarily pretty, but cute was a word she
could live with.

She pressed a towel to her face and rubbed it a little too roughly. Dan's
image appeared in the sparkles behind her eyes. He was handing her the
lily from his garden.

Benny's round, dimpled cheeks were rosy when she let the towel fall.
She ran a comb through her hair, pinned back the bangs growing out. The
aroma, conjured or real, of her mother's chicken cutlets made her belly
rumble. Sticking the ultrasound picture to the fridge, she ignored the little
voice telling her not to be so bold. She trotted down to her parents' place.
After dinner, she was going to make Clarice Grady a cup of tea. They
would sit out on the swing, sipping and chatting, exactly like they used to.

Chapter 12

Sing For Her An Elfin Mass

"Why so quiet, August?"

"I haven't much to say."

"That's a new one. For you."

"Be nice to me, Harriet. I am miserable. I have given Benedetta an impossible task, and only now that I've given it to her do I know how hopeless it is. I am doomed to this cemetery for all eternity."

"There are worst ways to be doomed."

"True enough. True enough. At least there are visits from Benedetta to look forward to."

"Until she's done grieving and doesn't come here anymore."

"Fanabala, woman, see what you've done? I am even more miserable than I was before."

"Well perk up, y'gobshite. Here she comes."

* * * *

The sky was overcast, and the temperature quite cold for late June, even in Bitterly. Benny wished she wore more than a hoodie to work. Tempted as she was to forgo the cemetery and get home early, she drove straight through town and out the other side. Augie would be waiting, she was certain.

Before she put the kickstand down, there he was. The sensation was akin to the concerned clicks of static electricity she had felt from Peter the night prior. Benny kept her eyes carefully averted. "It's okay, Augie. I'm not looking."

"Bene, bene. It is good to see you, Benedetta."

"Wow. You came right to the top of the pool, huh?"

Augie laughed, a good sound, and not like skittering leaves. "I am learning how to move faster, yes. And I have been anxious to see you."

"I have too," she said. "A strange thing happened last time."

"Stranger than listening to the tale of a man dead more than thirty years as told by a woman a century in the grave?"

"Actually, yes."

"Well then, I am curious. But what do you say we walk together, instead of sitting at your husband's grave or mine?"

"Walk?"

"Use your imagination, *cara mia*. I cannot feel the air or the sunshine, but I can move about and pretend."

"Then why did you have me chasing a wrapper the other day?"

"I have learned much since I first whispered my name to you," he said. "Like never doubt Harriet's word on anything."

"Such as?"

"Remembering." His tone sobered. "It used to be I could escape my shame by moving closer to life. I cannot any longer."

"Maybe that's a good thing. It probably means you're getting ready to move on."

"I had not thought of that."

Benny started walking, hands behind her back and head bowed. "I guess I fell asleep on you, huh?"

"You must have. Where you went, I could not follow."

"What do you mean? I was dreaming."

"Precisely." Augie asked her, "What did you dream?"

"I dreamed of Henny. He asked me to walk with him, and I didn't go."

Augie was silent long enough for Benny to wonder if he'd gotten pulled back to a deeper place, but he said, "A wise choice, *cara mia*. Life without him might be a sadder existence, but it is still life. As far as I know, it is the only one you will get."

Benny let that settle in. The crumbling walls of her secret were starting to let in light. Something like hope wriggled inside her, like Cricket did. Or maybe they were one in the same.

"Last thing I remember you saying to me," she said, "was you needed me to help you reach your daughter and beg her forgiveness on your behalf. Oh, and maybe introduce her to your children from your second marriage, if they are still among the living."

"My daughter, Adriana, was the youngest. She was born in 1945. She must still be alive, no?"

"She'd be..." Benny calculated. "About seventy. It's very possible. And you have no idea where she's living?"

"I can tell you where she was when I died. But..."

"But?"

"There was more to my story that I did not get to tell you, Benedetta. More to my shame than simply abandoning my child."

"Uh-oh." Benny halted. "Do we need Harriet?"

"Ah, no." Again his voice sobered. "As I said earlier, I now remember all too well. Have patience, *cara mia*, and I will tell my tale. But let us keep walking, so you do not fall asleep again."

* * * *

Augie told her about growing up in a small village within the vast Campania region of southern Italy, a happy boy who never dreamed of living anywhere else. Then came the Great War and harder times. He had been a child, but he remembered family and friends leaving their homes to travel across the sea—to America, where the streets were paved with gold. By the time he finally made the trip, he was a man of twenty, a husband and father, unhappy in the arrangement made for him before he took his first steps. When the opportunity to join an uncle overseas came, he took it.

"My wife, Carmen, I was happy to leave. If you could see me now, you would know I give the *maloik'* when I say her name. Nasty woman. But she loved our little Flora. At least, in this, I have no fear."

"What did you do when you got here?"

"Construction, like many Italians." He chuckled. "The country was still growing then. I took what work came my way, and sent every spare penny back home. After the Crash, it became harder and harder to send anything home. I grew thin in those days. My uncle and I lived with four other men in a tenement apartment meant for two. It was during this time Carmen decided I was good for nothing and invented my death so she could marry again."

"That must have hurt."

"It was a relief," he said. "My poor little Flora. I abandoned my child and it was a relief to know I would no longer need to send money I did not have. What sort of man does this?"

"But she didn't know that. She thought you died in America."

"This does not lessen my guilt."

Benny suppressed the urge to face him. It was strange, talking to someone without looking at him, seeing his facial expressions, his hand gestures. She imagined them, instead. And him. "Is this the more part?"

"It is."

"Worse than bigamy and abandoning a child?"

"You make it sound so sordid."

"Is it?"

"I suppose it is a matter of opinion, of course. But for me? Yes. Perhaps you should sit on the bench, right there."

"I'm okay walking."

"It might take a while to tell."

"You're stalling."

Birdsong. Footsteps. Traffic beyond the cemetery.

"Yes. I am. All right, Benedetta. I shall hope you will still help me after I've confessed my ultimate shame, for Flora's sake if not mine. You see, I found my daughter in Brooklyn. It was 1955..."

Augie told Benny of being discovered by an old friend from Italy, while in Yonkers on a job. He had become an accomplished builder by then. Word of mouth among *paesan'* sent him to New York often during the milder months.

"It was inevitable," Augie said, "being discovered alive and well in America. So many came from the Old Country, especially after the war. They mostly ended up in New York or New Jersey, working in construction of some kind."

President Roosevelt's New Deal provided hope as well as work. By the 1950s, Italian immigrants already there a decade or more were well established in the trades. Augie proved to his wife's pretentious family that a man with an accent wasn't a lesser being, but a man who could provide and provide well for his family, without their money or influence.

"They did not like me when I swept their daughter off her feet." Augie chuckled. "They forbid her to see me, then tried to stop our marriage. I was not only foreign, I was a Catholic. A heathen as far as they were concerned. But my Katherine, she was not like them. I could not have loved her if she was. She threatened to run away and never see them again, live in New York with all the miscreants. I did not know what the word meant, but I knew it was something awful, because her mother wept and her father relented. They even gave us property as a wedding gift. We both knew it was so Katherine would stay in Bitterly. It was okay. Neither of us really wanted to leave."

Augie's old friend told him of the family left behind in Italy who believed him dead, of his brothers forced to fight in the war. Only one of the three survived and, as far as he knew, still lived in the village in Campania. Carmen—her name accompanied by *maloik'*—also died during the war, the fate of too many women left to starve in the countryside, including Augie's mother. Flora would have starved as well if the old man Carmen married had not insisted on sending her, at the start of the war, to family he had in America. He, himself, only barely survived. He joined his beloved daughter—never stepdaughter—Flora when the war was over. By then, she had married, a good Italian boy who adored her. The last time his friend saw her, she had two little girls and another baby on the way. And though he had not been to their restaurant, On the Fire, in a while, as far as Augie's friend knew, they were still in Brooklyn.

"He told me she was very beautiful," Augie said. "For all her faults, I must admit that Carmen was as well. I did not give myself time to change my mind. I swore my friend to secrecy, got on a train and went to Brooklyn.

"It was an easy thing to find the restaurant. A very popular place. Meals were served family style, just like at home. The menu was whatever was cooking on the fire that day. My Flora cooked. Her husband, Anthony, played host. The children and, eventually, grandchildren served. Even the old man she called Papa had a job pouring wine he made himself. The moment I walked in the door, I was surrounded by family.

"I am not embarrassed to say I wept, Benedetta. Anthony came to me as if he knew, and in a way he did. I told him I had not felt home in many, many years. He said every *paesan'* who came had the same reaction when they first stepped through the door. A good man, my son-in-law. Kind and generous. My granddaughters brought platters of rabbit and vegetables and roasted potatoes. I ate my daughter's food and it was like eating my mama's again. Katherine, she never was a very good cook, but my Flora? A genius in the kitchen. Anthony insisted she come out of the kitchen and meet the new *paesan'*. I saw for myself her great beauty. It was like looking at Carmen on our wedding day, when I knew only what my eyes showed me and not what was to come."

"Was she really that bad?" Benny asked. "Or do you remember it worse, do you think?"

"She hit me," Augie said. "All the time. With a wooden spoon. She would lie in wait for me when I came home from work and knock me about the head, my back, my legs. Whatever she could reach as I ran from her. I believe she wanted me to hit her back, to give her reason to leave. She was an angry woman, Carmen was. Perhaps with reason. It was not an easy thing, being a daughter in so poor a village. She was given away, to me, when she was an infant. I wondered, had she been given a choice, if she might have loved me. Once she threw a brick through the window as I was coming up the steps and I knew then she never would, and for all her beauty and good cooking, I could not love a woman who hated me so much no matter how hard I tried. She was pregnant at the time, and Catholics were not permitted to divorce. There was no way out. At least, I believed there wasn't."

Augie fell silent. Benny continued walking, hoping he was still with her. She thought she could feel his presence, but whether it was him or his story causing goosebumps to rise, she wasn't certain until he spoke again. "My daughter kissed both my cheeks before I left. She let me hold her little son, a boy she named Alessandro Augusto after the father who raised her, and the one she had lost. I should have told her then. I should have taken her into my arms and begged her forgiveness. But I was a coward, Benedetta. She had such a happy life. A good life. The man who raised her had been devoted and loving. Who was I to step in and claim what was rightfully his?"

"That was a tremendous sacrifice, Augie," Benny consoled. "You did a noble thing."

"Perhaps if I was not also afraid to lose my own happy life in Bitterly, I might have allowed myself to believe this was true at the core. But I kept silent for myself, as much as I did for Flora. I was afraid I would lose Katherine, my children, the kind regards of her family I fought so hard to gain. I feared more than I loved, Benedetta. That is a great sin."

"Did you ever go back?" Benny asked. "To the restaurant?"

"Many times. Many times. Each time, I was greeted as an old friend. Once, when I went back after two years away, I learned the old man, Sandro, died. I could have told her then. When my in-laws died, I could have told her. When my children were grown, when Katherine died, so many times I could have told her. The more years that passed, the more impossible it became. Then it was too late. And now I am here."

"Oh, Augie." Benny wished to turn and hug him, to let him know with more than just words that her heart ached for his past. He was there, in her periphery. Just a blur. And a presence accompanied by the distinct sensation of being watched.

"Was that an, 'Oh, Augie, of course I will help you,' or an, 'Oh, Augie, you miscreant. Why would you ever think you deserved assistance?' Tell me, Benedetta, please."

"The first one."

Benny felt his relief as a physical thing. Breath on her neck. Electrical currents racing over her skin. She rubbed at her arms but the sensation remained.

"You've been dead a long time," she reminded him. "I doubt the restaurant is still there."

"But it will be remembered," Augie said. "Bensonhurst, Brooklyn."

"I know Bensonhurst. Kind of. I mean, I've been there. My mother's family is from there, originally. It's still very Italian."

"Ah, perhaps your mother remembers On the Fire. Or a relative will. It is a place to—"

"Benny!" Charlie's shout spun Benny to his voice, and there was Augie. No indistinct blur, but a spectral glow with features aghast and flickering. As if a gigantic hand grabbed her, four fingers clung, stretching, grasping, and losing purchase.

Sound crackled between her ears. Benny wobbled.

Augie was sucked away like a spider in the vacuum.

And silence.

Benny shook her head clear. Part of her saw Charlie coming her way, baby Valentine in his arms. Another part saw Augie swirling in a vortex back to the bottom of the pool.

"Augie?" she whispered. "Are you there? Augie?"

No answer. No presence Benny could even pretend to sense. Charlie was saying something, handing her the baby. Benny spoke words, later hoped she made no promises she wouldn't keep. The next thing she became fully aware of was riding slowly through the cemetery, taking the circuit twice. And though she tried first Henny's grave, then Augie's, he did not reappear.

* * * *

"You're a fool, August. Worse than a fool."

"How can I be worse than a fool?"

"You let her see you."

"I have never been so exhausted."

"Of course you are. You almost went out like a candle."

"Is that possible?"

"Sure it is. Seen it happen in my time."

"What happens, Harriet? To those who go out like candles?"

"Nothing good, Augie. Nothing good."

Chapter 13

She Murmurs Sleep

Benny chewed slowly. Her thoughts, as they had been these last days, on Augie. She went to the cemetery every day after work. Three days, and still no sign of him. Not even a whisper inside her head.

"I didn't mean to," she told Harriet one day, while tending her garden. "It was a reflex. If he can't come back because of me, I don't know what I'll do."

No reassuring pat on the shoulder. No presence or glow in her periphery. Just the silence of a cemetery where even ghosts kept to themselves. Her only consolation was, maybe, Harriet might be able to let Augie know she would do whatever she could to help him keep the promise he made to his daughter.

On this task, Benny had more success. A quick internet search showed her On the Fire still existed in Brooklyn. The proprietor was Tina Giadetti. The delicious-looking menu appeared a bit too extensive to still offer only whatever was on the fire, yet the black-and-white portrait embellishing the online menu and every page of the website was of a small, extraordinarily beautiful woman, her cheek pressed to that of a smiling, elderly man.

In the days since Augie's confession, Benny gathered information about the establishment itself, almost nothing on the people behind it. She had no idea what Flora's married name was, or if she'd taken her stepfather's name when her mother remarried. The name Fiore got way too many hits for her marginal internet skills, and calls to the restaurant were answered by staff that, wisely, would give out no personal information. She would have to go to Brooklyn herself, just as Augie had done all those years ago, and see what she could find firsthand.

Benny finished the *pastafazool* in her bowl and set it empty into the sink. Gone was the queasiness, as well as the heartburn. Her appetite lately was the stuff of legend, if one's goal was to win an eating contest. Her mother had eyed her with wary pleasure as she filled her second bowl.

"Thanks, Ma," she said. "Delicious, as always."

"Thank you, sweetheart." Clarice barely looked up from the pot she scrubbed. "You going upstairs?"

The hopeful tone in her mother's voice didn't escape Benny's notice. "Not unless you want me to make tea while you finish up."

"If you want. Sure. I won't be much longer."

She hadn't missed the hopeful tone, and neither did she miss the quickly quelled smile flash on her mother's lips. Benny put the kettle on, and took two mugs out of the cabinet. Irish breakfast tea for her mother, raspberry for her. Waiting for the water to boil, she leaned against the counter while Clarice tidied the kitchen.

Even as kids in need of chores to earn allowance, she and her brothers never got kitchen duties. This was her mother's domain, and she guarded it zealously. Filling the dishwasher, wiping down the counters, putting every pot and pan back into the right place was her religion. Aside from the occasional goodie-baking, cooking of any kind was a forbidden sacrilege. Food was her mother's medium, and she an artist of great skill and exacting temperament. Benny used to think her mother had some kind of disorder. In the course of her adult years, she came to understand it was pride. The kitchen belonged to Clarice Irene Grady, end of story.

The kettle whistled. Clarice wiped the last counter. Benny poured the tea, handed one to her mother and headed out to the swing. Sunset spread its last rays from behind the mountains, the trees. The day had been mild, and the evening was on the chilly side. Benny wished for her hoodie, but was too lazy to go upstairs and get it. Bats swooped at the rising insects. The mosquitos had already gotten her twice. Slapping at the spot, she told her mother, "I'm not sure how long I'm going to be able to stay out. The bugs are ridiculous."

"I have spray." Clarice held up the can, her finger on the button. Benny's hands shot up.

"No. Thanks. I can't stand the smell."

"Don't be silly. Would you rather be bitten? West Nile and all." Clarice moved closer with the insect repellant.

Benny leapt out of the swing, nearly spilling her tea. "I said no!"

"Goodness, Benny. No need to be sassy about it. Fine. Get bitten."

Clarice stepped away and doused herself with the repellant. Benny took slow, quiet breaths until her heart ceased its hammering, until she could stop picturing her Cricket with an arm growing out of her thigh, or sprouting a single eye in the center of her forehead, brought about by accidental exposure to bug-death-in-a-can.

"Peter leaves for Cape May tomorrow." Clarice blew across the top of her mug. "He seems excited."

"I'm a little jealous. I haven't been to the beach in years."

"You should go. It's not that far of a ride."

"It is on a scooter."

Clarice waved at the gnats circling her head. "You can borrow the car whenever you like. Or go with someone else who has a car."

Benny rolled her eyes. "Or a truck?"

"A truck would work, too. What about Johanna? I imagine she heads down to the Cape every once in a while to check on things. Hitch a ride with her. Or go with Savannah. You could probably both use a break from the farm. You have many friends in this town who would love to see more of you."

Benny pursed her lips. The kitchen might be her mother's domain, subtlety was not. "Someone like Dan Greene?"

"Now that you mention it…"

"Ma."

Clarice's burst of musical laughter surprised her. "Oh, settle down, Benedetta. You can't blame me for trying."

"Why do you even?" Benny grumbled. "This way you get to keep me here forever."

"Heavens, why would you say such a thing?"

Benny glanced up at her mother. "Isn't it what you want? To always have me and Peter here?"

Clarice patted Benny's knee. "Now that is what they call a double-edged sword, Benedetta. Of course I want you always with me. But I want you to be happy. Wherever and with whomever you wish. I mean that with all my heart."

"Then why are you always going on about Tim moving so far away?"

"Should I not miss my son?"

"I didn't say that." Benny slumped back in the swing. "But it makes him feel bad to think he's hurting you by living in North Carolina."

Clarice Grady sipped her tea, wiped the rim free of the rose-petal pink lipstick she always wore. "It is a fine line to walk, sweetheart, being a mother. Many fine lines, in fact. You tell me, Benny. What is worse? To have him feel bad that he lives so far away? Or have him feel bad that his mother couldn't care less he does? I let him know I miss him, but I don't hound him. If he feels bad, that's on him, not me. Right or wrong, it's my line. It's not so easy. You'll see. One day."

Benny opened her mouth to speak, then closed it again. She watched her mother out of the corner of her eye as she had learned to watch Augie. There was something about looking sideways that gave a perspective she'd never gotten before.

What others think of you is none of your business.

Where had she heard that before? Maybe her mother. Maybe some social media feed. It was nevertheless true. A lifetime of rebellion, six years of complacency—neither had as much to do with Clarice Grady as they did with Benny herself. Thought became thought. She lowered her mug. "Ma?"

"Yes, Benny?"

"I was wondering if you'd go with me someplace."

"Where to?"

"Brooklyn," Benny answered. "Didn't your family live there?"

"Bensonhurst, yes. Oh, my. I haven't been there in years. I think there might still be cousins in the area. Why do you want to go there?"

Benny considered lying, and settled for half the truth. "It's for a friend. An older guy I met at the cemetery one day."

"Oh? Who?"

"Just some old guy." Benny hedged around the truth. "He doesn't live in Bitterly. Relatives are buried here, though. He's looking for someone, his daughter, and has been a long time. The last he was able to track her down was a restaurant in Bensonhurst, but he can't travel so far. I thought, maybe, I could go into the city and see if I can find her, let her know he's looking for her."

"That's awfully nice of you, Benny."

"I feel bad for him. He's such a nice old man, and he feels…stuck. He says he made a promise to her and never kept it, and before he moves on, he wants to somehow keep it. When he mentioned Brooklyn, I remembered that's where you're from, and thought it would be a good opportunity for us to take a ride down."

"Really?" Clarice's eyes glistened. Benny hadn't the heart to tell her the idea only just came to her, even if it was sincere.

"If you want to, I mean. It's a long way."

"Not very. Three hours maybe. So. A restaurant? In Little Italy?"

"Isn't Little Italy in Manhattan?"

"Not if you're from Brooklyn." Her mother wagged a finger. "Just ask anyone in Bensonhurst. Do you know the name of the restaurant?"

"On the Fire. It's on—"

"On Eighty-sixth Street?" Clarice nearly dumped her tea. "Of course I know it. And you've been there. Well, not at the actual restaurant, but do you remember when we had Christmas Eve dinner with my cousin? You were eight or nine."

"Carmella?"

"You do remember."

"I was nine, and there were a gazillion people packed into her very small apartment. That was in Brooklyn?"

"It was, and my cousin is a terrible cook. The food came from On the Fire. It was my favorite place, once upon a time. Could it still be open?"

"According to the internet it is. So you want to go with me?"

"I would love to, Benny. But can we make it after the Fourth of July? I have so much cooking to do between now and then with the town picnic and contests. I am determined to win one of those blue ribbons this year."

"What are you talking about? You won three last year."

Clarice waved her hand. "Two for pies and one for bread. I've had my sights set on the meatball win ever since Addie Coco died, rest her soul, and Beanie D'Angelo moved to Florida."

"Your meatballs have always been at least as good."

"You're sweet, and maybe a little biased, but I agree. Let's see what the judges say this year."

Benny kissed her mother's cheek. "If they have any real taste-buds, the ribbon is yours. So, Brooklyn? How about the week after the Fourth? Any day but Wednesday. That's Savvy's only day off. I can't take another one."

Cold heat rushed to Benny's face, but if Clarice noticed her slip, she let it slide. "Monday's perfect. This is going to be fun."

"We can drive down to Southeast Station," she said quickly. "Take a train into the City."

"Or I could just drive."

"You? Drive all the way into the City?"

"What do you think of me, Benedetta?" Clarice shook her head. "Just because I don't leave Bitterly much doesn't mean I haven't, or I can't."

"I know. Sorry."

"I suppose it's my own fault, you kids thinking I have no interests outside my family and home. I do, Benny. Honest. I just keep it mostly to myself."

"Like what?"

"Oh, you wouldn't be interested in—"

"Ma."

"All right, all right." Clarice laughed that musical sound Benny couldn't remember hearing often enough. And though the bugs bit and the tea grew cold, Benny listened to her mother talk. About the family genealogy she'd been researching since college, an endeavor begun as a senior project and carried through her life. About the records from Italy that were nearly impossible to attain, and how she'd focused on the very small part of the family from England instead. About her mother's mother, Grace, who was English, making Benny less Italian than she was Irish despite identifying with her Mediterranean blood. Benny listened to every word, her heart itching and stitching to hear the passion in her mother's voice. It wriggled a little looser in her chest, dangerously closer to cracking open too wide for her to close up again.

Chapter 14

Its Twinkling Web

Loading lambs into their crates was sweaty work, but it was the last job of the day. The usually gentle critters wriggled and flailed. Benny got two in and was struggling with a third when Savannah shouted her name.

"Amber, take the lamb," she called one of the high school students, pulled Benny aside. "Are you nuts?"

"What?"

Savannah put her hands on her hips. Benny's face burned. "Oh, yeah. Dumb, huh?"

"Very. No lifting anything heavier than a small watermelon, especially if it has the potential to kick you." Savannah tucked an arm through Benny's, and started them toward the empty farmstand. "How are you feeling?"

"I'm fine. Why? Did you find something in the ultrasound after—"

"Relax, Ben." Savannah laughed softly. "Everything is fine with the baby, as far as I can tell. I'm talking about you. You okay? You seem distracted even for you."

Though she had not stopped in at the cemetery the last few days, there had been no sign of Augie. The trip to Brooklyn with her mother loomed. And as if the little cricket jumping around inside her wasn't enough to remind her of her responsibility to Dan, the ultrasound picture staring back at her from her fridge every single day did the job. Connected thoughts, feelings, worries and fears trailed after her from morning through night. Crowning it all was the town picnic and agricultural fair that kicked Savvy's into a frenzy of preparations, today being worst of all. The event itself would be a relief.

"There's just so much to do," Benny said. "And I still have to go home and dig out my camping gear for tonight."

"I told you, you don't have to stay with the animals," Savannah scolded. "The kids will do it."

"There are rules about having an adult on site for a reason."

"I guess you're right. I'm sorry I can't do it myself. They're my lambs. They just don't like me."

"Maybe because they know they're going to end up in your freezer."

"Benny, you're terrible." Savannah's laughter sobered quickly. Fingers to temples, she rubbed slow circles that made her face contort. "But maybe that's it."

Benny shooed a fly buzzing too close to her face.

Savannah's hands fell to her sides. "What are you doing?"

"This fly won't leave me be."

"What fly?"

Buzz-whiz-buzz-buzz-buzz. Benny yanked her hood up over her head. "It's gone. Don't worry about me or the lambs. It'll be fun."

"You'll call me if you need me, right?"

"Promise."

"I'll be there with breakfast, bright and early. I already put an order in at CC's for a dozen cinnamon chip scones."

"A dozen?"

"The kids'll eat them. And if they don't, more for us."

The farmstand was nearly empty. Moving the produce and preserves to the Green was a lot of work, but worth it. They'd sell it all. Always did. Not only did the whole town show up for the big picnic, but so did all the out-of-staters, their families and friends. It was Bitterly's most profitable day of the year.

"Looks like we're about done here," Benny said. "Anything else you need from me?"

"Nope. Go home. I'll have the kids unload everything and pitch the tent. You just show up."

"Eight o'clock?"

"No earlier."

"Yes, boss." Benny smiled, kissed Savannah's cheek and left the farmstand. She spotted a familiar truck in the gravel lot. Her stomach clenched but Benny didn't race to her scooter and drive away. Instead, she took a deep breath, let it go slowly, and approached the man loading bushel-baskets of potatoes into the bed of his truck. "Hey, Dan."

He spun, the potatoes in the basket flew out. He tried to grab them, lost his grip on the basket entirely, and the whole thing tumbled, potatoes rolling under his truck. Dan stared down at the mess, shaking his head. "I'll never get into Juilliard with those moves."

Benny laughed. "My fault, my fault. Let me help you."

"It's okay. I got this."

Benny helped him anyway. Dan's face was bright red from cheeks to ears, and though it might have been the heat, Benny was pretty sure it wasn't. He got down on his hands and knees to reach the potatoes under the truck, handing them up to her one at a time. Putting them into the basket resting on the tailgate, she tried not to notice his shirt riding up, the tanned muscles of his back, or that she knew the waistband poking out from his jeans belonged to boxers, not briefs.

"I think that's it." He rose to his feet, brushing off his hands. "Where were we before I tried to impress you with my grace?"

"I was just saying hello." Benny smiled up at him, squinting against the sunlight. "I don't have to ask if you'll be at the picnic tomorrow."

"Haven't missed one yet."

"Me either. Gads, does that mean we're old or boring?"

"Probably both."

She stuck her tongue out at him. It felt good. So good. Benny quelled the tremor scolding her. In her mind's eye, she placed a hand on her belly. In reality, she stuck it in her pocket.

"You going to be on the Green tonight," she asked, "keeping watch?"

"I have a shift, yeah. You?"

"I'm spending the night with the lambs."

"By yourself?"

"The lambs will be there."

He chuckled. "I guess I'll see you there, then."

Inside her head, Benny was hyperventilating. She inhaled and held it. "I'll make a thermos of cocoa, if you want to hang a bit," she exhaled the words, hoping she didn't sound as dizzy as she felt.

"It all depends?"

She blinked, the dizziness fading. Dan was smiling down on her, his pale-green eyes crinkling in the corners.

"On?"

"Whether it's the kind Johanna makes, or the crap they serve in the coffeehouse."

"The Johanna kind, of course."

"Then I'll be there. My shift is nine to midnight."

"Great." She patted the side of the truck as if it were a loyal dog, or a trusty steed. "I—uh—I'll see you later then."

Benny hurried off. Her heart fluttered in tandem with the little cricket wriggling in her belly, as if she'd known her daddy was nearby and was trying to out her mama. *Soon*, she told her unborn child. *I promise.*

Helmet on, Benny started her scooter and pushed up the kickstand. She resisted the urge to turn and wave, unsure if it was because she was afraid he'd be watching, or afraid he wouldn't be. Late afternoon stretched sunshine on the road ahead of her, bright and dappling through the trees. The wind kissed her face. Hope jiggled at the already-picked and mostly-dangling lock on her heart. And if luck was at all in sync with the moment, Johanna would have a few mud cookies left to go with the cocoa Benny would beg the recipe for.

* * * *

Teenagers piled into cars and trucks, balancing boxes and baskets of produce, jarred preserves, and even a crate full of ducklings on their laps. Somewhere in the background, Savannah shouted after them to wear seat belts, the big truck loaded with crated lambs rumbled to life. Dan Greene was still standing beside the tailgate of his pickup when silence fell and dust settled, wondering what in the hell had just happened.

"Everything okay, Daniel?"

He turned to Savannah's familiar drawl, afraid the smile on his face was the dreamy kind. He tried furrowing his brow, but the smile wouldn't quit. "I dropped some potatoes," he managed to say.

"I noticed." She pushed the basket into the truck bed and closed the tailgate. "I also noticed you talking to Benny."

"I noticed that too."

Savannah touched his arm, snagging his full attention. "Did she say something to stupefy you?"

"Yeah, she did."

"You going to expand upon that or leave me guessing?"

Dan shook off the lingering euphoria, attempting to smile without doing so stupidly. "She asked me if I wanted to hang out a bit tonight. She's making me hot cocoa."

Savannah's shoulders slumped. She rifled through the basket of potatoes as if she'd dropped something into it. "Well, that's nice. It's something, at least. A start."

"What? Did you think she propositioned me or something?" Dan snickered. "I'm a man of high moral standards, I'll have you know."

"A regular paragon of purity." Savannah backed away from the tailgate to look up at him, hands on her hips. "I'm glad she's talking to you again instead of running away. It's hard to keep quiet when people you love are hurting."

There was more. It was all over her face, in between words she didn't say. Dan had been one of the first to greet her when she first stepped foot in town, but Savannah Callowell was still a mystery he didn't think he had the skills to unravel. Whatever her thoughts, Dan let her keep them. He didn't have it in him to discuss Benny, what she meant to him, or all the contradictory emotions worming between them. She was making him cocoa. She wanted to 'hang a bit.' At the moment, it was all Dan's head had room for.

Getting out of his truck in his driveway, Dan didn't remember driving home. He had planned on going straight to the Green, to see if anyone could use his help. When he decided to go home and shower, he didn't know, but it was exactly what he was going to do.

"Evelyn?" he called as he stepped inside the house. It was unusually quiet and he remembered both the kids were staying with friends through the Fourth. It was a day both he and his sister pretended had no other significance than being the nation's birthday and Bitterly's most festive day of the year. Evelyn hadn't gone to the town picnic more than a few times since their parents' deaths. Dan had forced himself to go those first years, and thereafter wanted to again. His father had taken way too much from him. He'd not be taking the best day of the Bitterly year from him too.

Upstairs, Evelyn's voice, hushed and agitated, halted him in the hall. Dan walked quietly to her room. The door was open. He poked his head in. His sister held up a finger and he gave her privacy. In his own rooms above what used to be a garage and was now a family room, Dan relaxed. His own space, a quiet one where he didn't have to be funny or protective or all-around nice. Just a bedroom, sitting room, and his own bathroom— all the house he needed.

He showered, shaved, and even did more than towel-dry his hair. The curls he kept close-cropped were still thick and mostly blonde, though a darker shade than they used to be. His father had been bald on top by the time he was Dan's age, a fate he'd secretly feared most of his life. Dan was well aware he hadn't been the looker in their group of four as teens. Tim was the one all the girls went crazy for. Then Henny, and even ghostboy Charlie was ahead of gawky, goofball him. At forty, Dan considered himself not bad for an old guy, even if the still-blonder-than-blonde eyebrows over pale, green eyes made him look a little spooky. At least he was still in good shape. Last time he saw Tim, Dan schadenfreudely noticed a bit of a paunch.

"Daniel?"

"Hang on, Ev. I'm getting dressed."

His sister entered as he was pulling up his jeans. Dan turned his back quickly. "Jeez, Evelyn. I told you I was getting dressed."

"What's the matter? You grow something since the last time I seen you?"

Their mother's favorite one-liner. After all those years, he could still hear her mock-Italian accent when she said it.

"Matter of fact," he said. "Yeah. I have."

Evelyn smiled but she did not laugh. Dan held open his arms and she nestled into them.

"I don't want to think about it," she said into his chest. "About them."

"Then come to the picnic tomorrow."

"That only makes it worse. Paul's right, Dan. I have to get out of this town."

The mention of her ex-husband's name made him grimace. He put his sister at arm's length. "Is that who you were on the phone with?"

"He's coming to see the kids. And...and..." She stood up taller. "And me."

"You? Why you?"

Evelyn shrugged under his grasp.

"Evelyn. Why you?"

"Please don't start with me, Daniel."

"Start with you?" Dan let her go so he wouldn't shake her. "Are you forgetting what he did? How he abandoned you and the kids to go find himself with his twenty-four year old girlfriend?"

"He made a mistake. He said he's—"

"Sorry? He said he's sorry and that's it? Done? Forgiven and forgotten?"

"I didn't say I was taking him back," Evelyn said wearily. "Or that I will ever forget what he did. I just said he's coming to see me and the kids. And you don't know everything, Daniel."

"I know you got sick. I know he cheated. I know he took off for Colorado and barely sees his kids or provides for them."

"Those are all true. I don't deny it." Evelyn moved to the couch, patted the cushion beside her. "Come sit with me, okay?"

Dan's whole body fought obeying. For a split moment, he was twelve again, and his dad was calling him into the study. The hair on the back of his neck rose, but he went to his sister and sat beside her.

"I'm going to tell you something you don't want to hear," she said.

"Then why are you telling me?"

"Because you need to understand. Dan, listen. You never liked Paul much. He reminded you of dad, and—"

"He did not." But he did. Heat rose to Dan's face.

Evelyn took his hand in hers. "I didn't have the same relationship with dad you did. I'm not saying he was kind, or that he didn't smack you and mom around. I'm just saying I have a few more good memories than you do."

"Like?"

"Like he never missed a daddy-daughter dance with my Girl Scout troop?"

Dan shook his head.

"Paul reminds you of dad for a reason. He is like dad, in a lot of ways. But not all ways. He can be a jerk. I know it, and you know it. But he can also be really great." Her shoulders rose. And fell. "Dad had his issues. What they were, I couldn't say for sure. But Paul? He had it rough. As rough as you. And that's another reason why I fell for him in the first place. He reminded me of you."

"Damn, Ev. That's pretty gross."

"Don't joke. Not now."

Dan tried not to smile. He tried so hard. But it was all he knew how to do.

"He made more of an effort to save our marriage than I did," she continued. "I didn't want to do anything. I never wanted to go anywhere. We never had sex or even talked. I claimed I quit my job to stay home with the kids, but it wasn't true. Not really. I quit my job so when the kids went to school I could go back to bed."

"You were sick."

"I was. The Lyme disease masked the depression very well. I didn't realize it until I finally got the Lyme under control, and still never wanted to get out of bed."

Dan grimaced. "I thought the Lyme got so bad you couldn't—"

"It's what I wanted you to believe." Evelyn shifted to the edge of the couch, facing him. "That's what I wanted everyone to believe. It let me be poor Evelyn, whose husband left her because she was sick and he didn't want to take care of her. Poor Evelyn, whose brother had to move in to help her make ends meet. Poor Evelyn, who couldn't keep a steady job because she was always battling a disease people can understand and feel sympathy for. People don't understand depression, Dan. They don't get how debilitating it is, and it's not a matter of cheering up or, being tougher. Remember what Dad used to call Mom?"

A shiver raced up Dan's spine. His father's voice slithered out of the past. *Lazy bitch.*

Dan couldn't say the words. He didn't have to.

"It guts me to remember that I believed it myself sometimes," Evelyn said softly, "when she wouldn't get off the couch for days at a time. Remember?"

Dan remembered the bruises, too, and bringing ice wrapped in washrags for her eyes. He nodded.

"I was a stupid kid, and I was afraid. I sided with Dad because it was safer to be his ally than his enemy. I…I left it for you, Dan, and I'm so sorry."

"Don't," he said.

Evelyn grasped his hand. "But I am. So, so sorry things were the way they were, for not doing anything to stop it. There's way more to it, of course. That's why I've been working all this crap out since Paul left. And…" She bit her lip. "That's why I didn't go to the doctor when you made me call."

"You didn't?"

She shook her head. "But I did go to my psychiatrist and got my meds tweaked a bit."

"You have a psychiatrist?"

"I do. She saved my life, Dan. I was close to packing it in, after Paul left."

"No kidding. Why do you think I moved in here instead of just helping you pay bills?"

Tears welled in his sister's eyes. Her soft laughter trembled. "Why do we do this? Why do we always hide stuff from one another?"

"I don't think it'd take a genius to figure it out."

"True." She sighed. "Look, Paul is no saint, but our problems started with me. He made bad choices. He acknowledges it. I'm not saying he's going to come back here and all will be well, but I am keeping an open mind. I hope you can, too."

Dan folded his hands in his lap, concentrated on his thumbs as if they might wander off if he didn't. "What about his girlfriend?"

"Bonnie?" Evelyn waved her away. "She split on him as soon as they got out there. He was her way out of Connecticut, nothing more. Apparently, Colorado was her idea in the first place. Legal pot."

"Ouch. That had to have knocked his dick right out of his pants, eh?"

Evelyn flopped back into the couch cushions, snickering. Her expression softened, turned sad. She looked so like their father and, sometimes, it made him wince. "I won't pretend it didn't give me a happy little giggle, at the time. He was humiliated, but he told me. He didn't have to."

"I guess it's something," he murmured. "Do the kids know he's coming to see them?"

"Not yet. I'll tell them when they come home. Joss will be happy, but Mabel's been really pissy where he's concerned."

"She's at that age." He shrugged. "Her dad didn't just leave her, but left her having to be driven around in a crappy minivan instead of a Land Rover."

Evelyn pursed her lips. "We spoiled them both. Overcompensation? Probably. But Paul's not making anywhere near what he did here. He opened a shop in Boulder."

"A shop? What kind of shop? Smoke shop? And, if so, could he hook me up with—"

Evelyn swatted at him. "Sporting stuff, you goofball. He does skis and snowboards in the colder months, bikes and skateboards in the warm ones."

"Paul?" Dan shook his head. "Power-tie-wearing, executive-type Paul Tyler?"

Evelyn swatted him again, but she smiled. "He's done a lot of changing the last few years. But he seems happy."

"That's good. I guess."

"It is. I'm glad for him. And I'm kind of nervous about seeing him, to be honest."

"The hell? Why?"

"I just am. And I'm done talking about this now, okay? I just wanted you to be aware that he's coming."

"He staying here?"

"Not if you don't want him to. This is your house now, not his."

"How about if you want him here, I do too, and if you don't, I'll toss him out on his hippie ass before he can tell me to chill?"

She sat forward on the couch, elbows resting on her knees. "Sounds good. Thanks, Dan. And sorry for walking in on you and...Mr. Johnson."

"It's all right. Mr. Johnson was tucked away by then." Dan got to his feet. "I have a shift down on the Green tonight, keeping the peace. I'll be back around twelve. Will you be okay here by yourself? No getting rid of everyone so you can check out, right?"

"If I was going to off myself, I'd have done it by now," Evelyn said without batting an eye. "I'll be fine."

She held out her hands. Dan grabbed them and hoisted her to her feet.

"Have a good night, Dan," she said, walking backwards out of the room. "And say hi to Benny for me."

Dan shook his head, grinning like a madman. Whatever they hid from one another, Evelyn knew him better than anyone else in the world. Dan wished she didn't, because, in light of all she'd told him, he had to accept that he didn't know his sister at all.

Chapter 15

Kisses Cool of Drowsy Mist

Cocoa still warm in the thermos, cookies in a waxed bag tucked in her backpack, tent set up and lambs bedded down for the night, Benny was ready. Maybe. She believed she was. And then Dan's booming laughter came from somewhere outside the enclosure and her belly flipped right up to her throat. "You can do this," she muttered. "Once it's done, you'll feel better."

Only she wouldn't feel better, because it was just the beginning of a whole other set of problems way bigger than telling a man she slept with he was going to be a father.

Footfalls in the grass. A silhouette on the side of the tent, and then the deep and familiar voice that made her heart flutter. "Benny? You in there?"

"In by the lambs," she called.

Now those footfalls swooshed in the grass between the two-person tent she would sleep in to the bigger one for the sheep. A beam of light preceded him. Benny shielded her eyes.

"Why you sitting here in the dark?"

"It's peaceful," she said.

He flashed his light on the lamb enclosure. "They sure are cute. Too bad they're so delicious."

"I don't eat baby animals."

"Do you eat eggs?"

"Of course."

"Aren't those just pre-babies?"

"Pre-babies?" Benny shook her head. "Why are we discussing this?"

Dan blew a breath through his lips and rubbed the back of his neck. "Because I am nervous as a bull-calf at a Rocky Mountain Oyster Festival. Can I start again?"

"Sure."

Dan left the enclosure, stood silently outside of it a moment, then called, "Benny? You in there?"

"In by the lambs," she called, more softly than she did the first time, but he came in with his flashlight all the same.

"Hey, Benny."

"Hey, Dan."

He flashed the light on the lambs. One bleated. Dan smiled. "They all settled in for the night?"

"Not much to do but make sure no one gets swiped during the night. I have a couple of chairs outside, and a thermos of cocoa. The Johanna kind. What do you say?"

"I say let me give you a hand up."

Benny took the hands he offered. Big and strong and calloused hands. Hers felt good, resting in his, and she only let one of them go when she was on her feet. Dan seemed surprised, but he didn't let go either, rather, led her through the dark enclosure to the moonlit, star-splashed night outside.

"It's chilly out here." She rubbed at her arms. "I can't believe it's July."

"Feels like September. Want my jacket?"

"No, thanks. I have one. Wait here."

Benny ducked into her tent and grabbed her hoodie, pulling her arms into the sleeves as she backed out. Dan was chuckling.

"What?"

"You still have that ratty sweatshirt?"

She flipped up the hood and brandished the Grim Reaper logo on back. "Until death do us part. It's my favorite thing."

"I remember."

"What do you remember?"

Dan gestured her into one of the folding chairs before taking the other. Benny poured him cocoa from the thermos, and handed him a cookie.

"You thought you were hot shit in school," he said, "wearing that jacket."

Benny swatted at him. "I was."

"As long as you think so."

"You don't?"

"Nope." He took a huge bite of the cookie. "You were always Tim's baby sister. Total dork. But you sure were cute, wearing your bad-ass hoodie like you were the coolest girl in school."

"Guess I wasn't fooling anyone, huh?"

"I give you an A for effort, though. All that black. And the makeup thing. What was it? From a movie, I think."

"The Crow."

"Right, right. Never saw it."

Benny grimaced, chagrined. "Neither did I."

"You're kidding."

"Nope. I was a kid trying to be unique."

"You didn't need movie-makeup to be unique." He leaned forward, elbows on knees. "Would it be shallow of me to say I like being able to see more of your pretty face?"

"Why would it be shallow?"

"Because it's what's on the inside that counts."

"Well, yeah," she said. "But everyone likes to hear she's pretty to someone."

"It doesn't make me shallow? Because I do think you're pretty, Benny. Beautiful."

Benny's heart stuttered. Leaning on his elbows, his expression open and his eyes hopeful, he was like a little boy looking for approval instead of a forty-year old man trying to win a woman over. Henny used to tell her she was beautiful. He would say it and Benny felt it down to her bones. But Henny was gone, and Dan was there, looking at her with those gentle eyes.

Let him in, Benny. Let him in.

For a moment, Benny thought the voice in her head was Augie. It felt exactly as his did, when he was deeper in the pool. But it wasn't. She knew it wasn't Henny's either, and while she couldn't swear it wasn't Harriet's, she was pretty sure it was her own.

All right, she told that voice, *I will. I'm sorry, Henny. I'm sor—*

She cut herself off there. Chasing off the ghost in her head wasn't easy, but she leaned forward, as Dan was leaning forward.

"Thank you." Benny's heart welled. Her stomach clenched. She ran her fingers along his jaw. "I think you're kind of beautiful, too."

"I've got spooky eyes," he blurted.

"I like spooky."

"But do you like me?" He flopped back in his chair, snickering. "How incredibly middle-school, huh? Do we ever outgrow it?"

"We like to think so. But the answer is yes, Dan. I do like you." She grinned. "I like you, like you."

She hoped to make him laugh. Dan blew out a deep breath instead. "I get it, Benny. Henny and all. I'm not as dumb as people think."

"I never thought you were dumb."

"A goof then."

"Well, you are that."

Dan sat forward again, this time taking her hands. "I kind of hoped the reason you pulled away was because you felt something for me you weren't ready for."

"That has a lot to do with it."

"Are you ready now?"

"I might be," she said. "I'm trying to be."

"Do you want me to fight for you, Ben? Or do you want me to leave you the hell alone? Just tell me which it is. I might not listen, but at least I'll know."

"I don't want you to fight. And I don't want you to leave me alone." *Just be.* Harriet's words, through Augie, whispered inside her head. "We're both thinking too much, because we both loved Henny. Let's just be, Dan. Whatever we are, however that turns out. Okay?"

"Okay."

Inside the enclosure, a lamb bleated. Then another, and then all of them in chorus. Benny and Dan turned to the sound, rose to their feet. Dan shined his flashlight inside and Benny ducked under his arm for a closer look.

"Nothing," she said to Dan coming up behind her. "I swear, one of them gets bored and starts the rest of them going just so he has something to do."

"Not a bad plan." He swiped the beam of light over the whole flock, stopping at the one with black spots on his face. "That's the one, right there."

"You think so?"

"He's got bad boy written all over his face."

"He looks sweet to me."

"Take my word for it," Dan said. "I know sheep."

And she knew bad boys. Henny was. And so was Augie. But the lamb wasn't, and neither was Daniel Greene.

As she stood looking down at the lambs, her mind turning and tumbling over itself, Dan's arms encircled her from behind. His chin rested on her shoulder. "Is this all right?" he whispered into her ear, kissed the tender spot just below.

Benny nodded. She leaned into him. There they remained for hours, or moments. The cool humidity of a July night in the Berkshire Mountains enveloped them as Dan did her. His hands rested gently on her abdomen. Cricket jumped and bumped but he didn't seem to notice. Benny closed her eyes, came so close to telling him. This time, her silence came from hope, not fear.

"You want to go to the picnic with me tomorrow?" he asked.

"Well, we'll both be here, won't we?"

"I was hoping for more than saying hi as we pass one another at exhibits."

"More? As in having lunch together?"

"Maybe ride a few rides?"

"Will you buy me cotton candy?"

"I might be persuaded to break open the piggy bank."

Benny turned in his arms, winding hers around his neck. "What would I have to do to persuade you?"

"Love me?"

The muscles in his arms twitched.

"I didn't mean—"

"I know what you meant, Dan."

"I'm not good at this kind of thing. My mouth starts flapping before my brain gets a chance to shut it the hell up."

"Dan." Benny placed a finger upon his lips. "How about your brain shuts it the hell up now so you can kiss me?"

His smile burst like light in the dark enclosure. Dan was right. His eyes were spooky. And beautiful. And beloved. Chills raced along her skin, into her blood and bones. Her heart thrummed to a new beat, one only this man could call up. Benny lifted her chin, closed her eyes, kissed him as he kissed her. Dan gathered her closer. She pressed her body to his. Between them, their child danced her little cricket dance, to her daddy's newborn tune, and tears welled. Benny let them fall so the joy would not overwhelm. She was suddenly, euphorically happy she hadn't told him yet. There were a thousand and one wonderful ways she might. In her mind, she was already planning how she would.

"I'm supposed to be keeping the peace," he said between kisses. "You're making me shirk my responsibilities."

Benny kissed him one more time, and let him go. "It's probably best if you go now, anyway," she said. "I wouldn't want to ruin your reputation."

"Scandalous." He caught her hand. "So will you go to the picnic with me?"

"I'd love to."

"I always watch the fireworks with my mom," he said. "I know that sounds strange but…"

"Look who you're talking to."

"Oh, yeah. Do you mind?"

"Sounds perfect. In fact, I was going there to visit a friend tomorrow. It's his birthday."

Dan lowered his gaze. Benny opened her mouth to ask what was wrong, but he looked up again, smiling. "Then it's a date." He offered his arm, back stiff and pinky raised. "Now, Miss, if you would do me the honor, I shall escort you home."

"Most certainly, kind sir." Benny took his arm and they walked regally through the dark enclosure, to the moonlit and star-splashed night outside. At the zipped-up tent, Dan took her arm from his elbow and kissed her fingertips. "Thanks for the cocoa. And the cookie."

"Take what's left for your watch," she said. "I'm going to sleep."

"I will, thanks."

Dan unzipped her tent, gestured her gallantly inside. Benny kissed his cheek as she slipped by him. Sitting on her heels atop her sleeping bag, she waved to him through the flap.

"I'll check in on you before I leave the green," he said, his hand on the zipper to close her in. "Make sure none of the delinquents in town shave-cream your tent while you're sleeping."

"No, don't." She laughed. "I snore."

"I know," he said, and zipped the flap closed. Benny flopped backwards, covering her eyes with her arm and letting the happiness fill her. Outside her tent, Dan whistled as he walked away.

Chapter 16

Each Wildflower's Heart

Night never lasted so long. His shift on the Green ended at midnight, but Dan hadn't gone right home. Half an hour with Benny had juiced him up like twelve cups of Cuban coffee. He stayed until two, talking with the attendant watching over the amusements, joking with old friends, checking in on Benny snoring away in her tent. Dan imagined her, wrapped up in her ratty hoodie, and had to force himself not to unzip the flap and crawl in there with her. He'd pushed too hard, too fast once. He wasn't making the same mistake twice.

At home, he looked in on Evelyn—just in case—and went to bed. Half an hour later, Dan was still wide awake. He showered, got back into bed, but whenever he closed his eyes, he was kissing Benny again, feeling her body pressed to his, her arms around his neck, her hands in his hair. The itch under his skin became a burn. He got back into the shower, but cold water didn't banish the burn, and taking care of the burn didn't banish the itch. As dawn lightened the sky and he was about to give up, slumber finally fell on him. Hard.

"Hey." A familiar voice. A hand smacking his butt. "Big man. Aren't you supposed to be grand marshalling some tractor pull at the picnic?"

Dan lifted his groggy head, blinked away the dream just as it was getting good.

"Dan. Wake up. You're late."

He bolted upright, grabbed his cell. After ten o'clock, and three missed messages. Scrolling through them, he blew out a relieved breath. Nothing from Benny telling him he needn't bother to find her if he couldn't be on time. They were all from Charlie, who filled in for him at the registration booth for the tractor pull, but had to jet because Johanna was judging the pie-baking contest and if he missed it, he'd end up in her next batch of shepherds-pie-pies.

"Dammit," he grumbled, tossing aside the sheets and texting Charlie back.

"Dan, gross. Cover that thing, will you?"

"Huh?" He glanced down. "Oh, sorry." He thumped into the bathroom and turned on the hot water in the sink, calling, "Can you toast me a bagel or something while I get ready?"

"Sure. How'd it go with Benny?"

Dan stuck his half-lathered face out of the bathroom. "She's going to the picnic with me today. I have to buy her cotton candy though. That was the deal."

"Make sure you check your bank balance before swiping your card for that one." Evelyn chuckled at her own joke and started away.

"You okay, sis?" Dan asked. She turned back.

"I am, Danny. Thanks."

Danny. His heart did a little flip in his chest. Only his mother ever called him Danny, and only at home. He nodded to his sister and she smiled in return before leaving him to his preparations. In twenty minutes, he had to be in Young's Field just north of the Green to oversee the tractor pull. Thankfully, he still had Benny's cell number stored in his phone. He hoped she had hers on her.

Slept late. All your fault...

He blew out a breath. Delete. Delete. Delete. Funny was safe. Benny deserved better than safe.

Overslept. Was dreaming of you. Will see you at the food concessions for lunch after the tractor pull. ??

As he thundered down the steps to the kitchen, his cell buzzed.

Glad to know you think of me, pal. Hope there was no sock involved in that dreaming. If there was, you at least owe me dinner.

Dan checked the number. Charlie's not Benny's. He forwarded the first message to her before he lost his nerve, then, snickering softly to himself, he texted Charlie back.

I need two socks for you, buddy. Make sure Benny got the message I just sent her, will you?

Will do.

Dan tucked his cell in his pocket, sailed through the kitchen and grabbed the toasted bagel Evelyn was holding out to him. Backing down the driveway, he almost ran into an unfamiliar car. It stopped. Dan honked and waved but the car backed up and the driver waved him out. Nondescript sedan. Out-of-state plates. An obvious rental. In his rearview, as he pulled away, the car turned into his driveway. "Shit."

He slammed his palm against the wheel, but Dan didn't turn back.

* * * *

Overslept. Was dreaming of you...

She felt like a teenager getting a note from her secret crush. Until reading Dan's text, Benny hadn't realized she was waiting for it. For him. She'd been up since dawn with the bleating lambs and Savannah's delivery of fresh scones from CC's. She checked the program listing for the tractor pull. It started at eleven. No end time. Though she told herself 'lunch at the concessions' was too vague a time for her grumbling belly, the lie didn't convince the thrills chasing over her skin. Benny couldn't wait to see him. She wanted to see his smile bloom when he saw her. She wanted to feel that amazing tumbling in her belly when she saw him. It was a beautiful day, and she was so full of hope, Benny was pretty certain she could shoot sunbeams and rainbows from her fingertips if she tried.

"Savvy, if you don't need me, I'm heading over to the tractor pull."

"You've done enough," Savannah said. "Go. I've been telling you to go for hours."

Benny tossed her hoodie into the tent she left up, grabbed her helmet, and started for her scooter. The deep furrow of Savannah's brow stopped her short. "Again? These headaches are getting way more frequent, Savvy."

"It's only my allergies are starting early," Savannah answered. "It'll pass."

"You know it's not allergies," Benny scolded. "You've been getting them for as long as I've known you. And they're getting worse."

A buzzing careened around and through Benny's head. She swatted at it. "Damn. What was that?"

"Another fly?"

"They give me the willies. That buzzing goes right through me." She shook it off, then, "Please go to the doctor."

"I've been. Before I ever came to Bitterly. I have a friend, back in Georgia, a neuro-surgeon who worries about me even more than you do. She couldn't find anything wrong, and believe me, she looked. But I'll take something for it, okay?"

"Okay. I guess."

"Go enjoy the tractor pull." Savannah kissed her cheek. "And your day with Dan."

Instead of recoiling and hushing her as she would have a week ago, Benny waved and dashed to her scooter, leaving her boss's headache and the willies behind her.

Though Young's Field was no more than a few minutes from the Green, it took Benny twice what it should have to get there. As sleepy a town as Bitterly was most of the time, events like Village Harvest Fair, the carol sing at Christmas, and the Fourth of July brought in every resident, full and part time, as well as visitors from the surrounding area. She contemplated riding on the sidewalk or weaving between cars, but Benny didn't have it in her to be so reckless these days. Henny wouldn't have thought twice about it. And look what it got him.

She gasped, scolding the unkind, angry voice in her head, as if made any difference. Anger was an uncalled-for emotion, considering the price he paid. It didn't stop these angry bursts now and then, though, or the fact that it felt good to be angry with him. Parking her scooter at the far end of the field, she tried to remember the combination to the lock she almost never used. She walk-trotted to the announcer's booth, leaving Henny's ghost determinedly behind. She conjured Dan, of how he made her laugh, of how he made her feel safe and special and beautiful, of how she would tell him about their baby before the day was done.

She spotted his blonde head in the announcer's booth, a microphone to his lips. His words crackled static. "Virgil Morris, get your dog off the field!"

Benny craned her neck to see over the crowd, and got a glimpse of Virgil Morris the younger struggling to get the dog off the tractor tire he was trying very hard to kill.

"Guess we ought to be glad he's ferocious and not amorous," Dan said into the mic. "Kids, make sure to ask your parents what that means when you get home."

Groans and laughter rose up from the crowd. Benny shouldered her way to the booth just as the tractor engine roared to life. Dan didn't see her climb over the side of the booth or slip up behind him to put her arms around his waist.

"Holy sh—" He turned in her arms without stepping out of them. "You're here."

"I'm here," she said over the tractor engine and the cheering. His happiness was surprised, and sincere. Benny wanted to kiss him so badly. *Just be, Benny. Just be.* So she did.

Dan stiffened and relaxed almost in the same moment. Benny smiled against his lips. She did not care who saw them or what they thought, or repeated. Reclaiming this small, rebellious piece of herself she believed lost allowed her to melt into him when his hands came up to cradle her face. Only when he drew reluctantly away did Benny realize the cheering had shifted from the tractor already done with its pull to them. Dan blushed, grabbed the mic and called into it, "I got a little distracted there. Nancy, how far was the pull?"

More laughter, cheers and good-natured ribbing. Benny relaxed. No one thought ill of her, or of Dan, after all. Everyone in town had loved Henny, their resident bad-boy who was really a nice boy who sometimes did crazy things. But the long-time residents loved her too, and Dan Greene was as close to a local icon as anyone could get outside of Charlie McCallan. It had never been their approval she feared getting.

"I see you couldn't wait for lunch."

Benny startled, hand to her heart. For one, split moment, she believed it was Augie, but the voice had been female, and it belonged to Johanna Coco McCallan.

"Didn't mean to scare you."

"It's okay." Benny leaned closer so she wouldn't have to shout over Dan and the growling engines. "I was daydreaming."

"I'd be too after that kiss. I thought you two called it quits last winter."

"It didn't stick."

"Good." Johanna peeked over Benny's shoulder, smiling in Dan's direction. "Now I can tell you how heartbroken he was when you stopped talking to him. He moped like Caleb did when he and his girlfriend broke up."

"Did he?"

Johanna nodded. Benny bit her lip to keep from smiling, and failed. "It's been so long since I felt this way. It's kind of scary."

"Love usually is."

Love. The word sent willies up Benny's spine all over again, a good kind this time. Henny's ghost, the one that wasn't actually Henny at all, rose up. Benny closed her eyes and forced it back.

"So," she changed the subject, "where's your littlest angel?"

"Back at the house with her Aunt Emma," Johanna answered. "We're taking shifts. I'll go home and get her later, once all the judging is done. This is all a bit too much for Valentine. And for me." She leaned in. "We're having another one."

"What?" Benny climbed over the side of the booth and threw her arms around Johanna's neck. "Another baby? When?"

"Shh!" Johanna hushed her playfully. "We haven't really told anyone yet. Yes, another one, in November."

"Me t—" Benny caught herself, tried to cover and only sputtered, "Meet you at…the…um…"

Johanna grabbed her arm and hauled her to a relatively quiet spot behind the sound system equipment. "Benny? A baby?"

"You can't say anything."

"I won't." She leaned closer. "Dan?"

"Of course." Benny shushed her. "He doesn't know yet."

"Well, I figured. There's no way he would have kept it a secret. So, did he knock you up on Valentine's Day like Charlie did me?"

"Johanna!"

"Well? It was Dan's fault, really. We were supposed to get that carriage ride, and instead he took you, and Charlie and I ended up in the woods behind the house, recreating the past."

Benny bit her lip. "Yeah. Valentine's Day."

"Then you stopped seeing him shortly after."

"I didn't know about"—she gestured—"you know, until a couple months later. It was the one and only time, Jo. He told me he was falling in love with me. I freaked out a little. A lot." Benny blinked back tears. If the tears started, they wouldn't stop. She was tired of crying, tired of being sad, tired of feeling guilty for living, for wanting to live, for loving someone who wasn't Henny.

Johanna pulled her gently into her arms. "I get it, hon," she whispered into her ear. "I do. I can't even begin to tell you."

She pulled gently from Johanna's embrace. "It has been so hard, but I am determined. There's more reason than myself to let it all go."

"Don't let it go for your baby, Ben." Johanna kissed her cheek. "Let Henny go for you."

Her words echoed Peter's, spoken days or weeks or years ago. Good advice, no matter how difficult. Advice Benny had every intention of heeding. Starting today.

* * * *

The tractor pull ended. Johanna left her to find her husband and the kids. They all met up at the finish line of the annual bike race to cheer Charlie's eldest son, Will, over the finish line. He came in a respectable third place.

"I should have taken second place," Will grumbled amid their congratulations. "Brian bumped me, back on the last curve."

"Dude! It was an accident."

The grin on Brian's face, familiar and wicked but not mean-spirited, dispelled any concern of an altercation. Though most of the immediate Fredricks family had moved out of town after Henny died, Brian was a cousin somewhere down the line. She remembered thinking, a long time ago, how history repeated itself. Will the good guy, Brian the bad boy, they were Charlie and Henny all over again. She gave the young man a gentle shove. His smile turned mischievously bashful, just like Henny whenever he was caught out, and Benny just wanted to hug him.

On the way to the concessions for lunch, they passed through the tents where the food contests were judged. She spotted the blue ribbon on her mother's berry pie and a yellow on her braided bread. The meatball contest wouldn't be judged until later in the day, but there was Clarice Irene Grady, hovering over her fare like a mother hen over her eggs. She waved and winked, gave a not-very-subtle thumbs up in Dan's direction before shooing Benny along.

Finding a place to sit and eat wasn't hard. Charlie and Johanna were unacknowledged king and queen of the picnic. Space emptied the moment they were spotted, joking shouts for Mayor McCallan making Charlie blush and Johanna nudge him in a see-I-told-you manner. Benny hugged herself about the waist, absorbing the general mayhem and good feeling too long absent, too long ignored. Happiness filled her so full nothing else could get in, not even when Dan went to get her the promised cotton candy and Charlie hugged her hard and tight.

"She told you," Benny accused.

"Of course she did. Now you have no choice but to tell him, because I'm not going to be able to keep this secret long."

Benny kissed his cheek. "You squeal and I'll bite you good."

"Promise?"

"Charlie!"

He lifted her off her feet and twirled her once. "Welcome back," he said close to her ear, and set her on the ground again just as Dan returned with the cotton candy and an unconvincing glare.

While the two men mock-battled over her, Benny drifted out of herself. All the months of avoiding him, avoiding telling him, whirred like dust in a summer wind. In this soundless joy, Dan left off battling Charlie to gather her to him, his arms around her waist and his chin resting on her shoulder. In this fragile moment between then and now, Benny stopped herself from moving his hands to her abdomen and letting the hardness of it tell him for her. She wanted it to be something they'd both remember all their lives, after all. But she didn't.

When their car stopped on the top of the Ferris Wheel, Dan put his arm around her and pulled her in close. He rested his head to hers and everything welling inside of him washed into her, became the same sensation passing back and forth, back and forth. He tilted her face up, his pale eyes gobbling down every word in her head. A tender kiss lit Benny's insides, burned through her so that it was not enough. They kissed on the top of the Ferris Wheel, as it went round and round. At last the ride stopped and they broke apart reluctantly, only slightly self-consciously, and all thought of doing anything but getting back to his lips went the way of the summer breeze.

Hand-in-hand, Benny and Dan strolled to the judging tents and waited for the results of the meatball contest. Her mother came in second. Though she held up her red ribbon and smiled triumphantly, Benny knew her disappointment cut deep. Instead of insisting they help eat the meatballs still left in the pot, Clarice said she was going home to wash up before the fireworks started, and refused Benny's help.

"You have fun and leave your mother to her pouting," Peadar Grady told his daughter. "She'll be just fine."

After another mayhem-meal with most of Bitterly at the concessions, Benny thought she would tell Dan about the baby on the ride to the cemetery, but it was probably best not to give him the news while he was driving. During the fireworks, she decided, and was content. As he pulled through the gates, Benny realized she hadn't been to the cemetery in a few days, and hadn't even thought about it or Augie in passing. Too happy to feel guilty, she nonetheless closed her eyes and listened hard.

"What?"

Benny opened her eyes. "What, what?"

"You just sighed."

"I'm happy."

Dan took her hand and squeezed. "Me too."

"You mind if I make a visit before we go sit with your mother?"

"Not at all."

Dan slowed at the same tree she always parked beneath. Benny wouldn't go to Henny's grave this night of all nights. Even the thought was enough to wiggle loose the chinking of her present happiness.

"Not here," she said. "Go past your mom's grave, to the old section by the woods."

He opened his mouth as if to speak, but he only nodded and continued through the cemetery. He stopped the truck in the exact right spot, turning off the engine.

"Give me a moment first, okay?"

"Sure, Ben." He grinned big. "Go break up with your boyfriend."

Benny cocked her head, her mouth dropping open as memory kicked in. "Oh, jeez. You knew?"

He nodded sheepishly. "I was here one day, helping Charlie with the sprinkler system. I saw you over here, and did some snooping."

"You mean stalking."

"Hey, I was worried. You were acting strange." He tapped her nose with a big, square finger. "Even for you."

"Ha-ha." She stuck her tongue out at him. Leaning across the seat, she kissed Dan quickly. "Two minutes," she said, and bolted out the door.

He wasn't there. Not in any depth she could feel him, anyway. She stood silently still at his gravesite, reading the epitaph—

Katherine Weller Fiore
September 13, 1919 ~ January 28, 1976
*

August Fiore
July 4, 1908 ~ July 7, 1980

"Happy Birthday, Augie," she whispered. "I hope you can hear me. I'm here with a friend. His mom rests"—She turned and pointed—"right up there. We're going to watch the fireworks with her. He does it every year. So, see? I'm not the only one who hangs out with the dead.

"I'm sorry. I've said it a bajillion times, but I am. I miss you, Augie. And I miss hearing from Harriet through you. Did you make her up just to make me happy?" She sighed. "I'm going to New York with my mom on Monday. I'll find Flora, or find out about her, and I'll help you keep your promise. I swear it."

From the truck parked at the side of the cemetery road, Dan waved to her.

She waved back, waved him over.

He got out of the truck and came her way.

"I want you to meet Dan," she told the tombstone. "He lives in the house you built. Did Harriet tell you he still has the concrete with your kids' handprints in it? I asked her to."

Still nothing. She couldn't even pretend.

Footfalls on the dry grass, then Dan's arm slipped across her shoulders. "So this is my competition, huh?"

Benny nudged him. "I've been told he was very handsome."

"He's also very dead. I'm pretty confident I'm better looking at this point. I'm positive I smell better."

Benny laughed. "He's the man who built your house."

"Ah, right. August Fiore built it for his Weller bride, yes. I didn't know he was a friend of yours." Dan glanced up at the sky. "Much as I like meeting your friends, it's getting dark. The fireworks are going to start any minute."

"Oh, sorry." Benny touched Augie's gravestone. "I'll be back."

She took Dan's outstretched hand, and, glancing once behind, followed him back to the truck.

* * * *

"He is her lover. I can tell."

"So?"

"Sew buttons. You know how I feel about her."

"August Fiore, you are so dead she can't even feel you standing right next to her. What right do you have to say anything about her taking a man as her own?"

"Plenty. If only I could…"

"Could what?"

"Harriet?"

"What now?"

"You don't go any closer to the living, but you can, isn't that so?"

"Don't go getting any ideas, Augie."

"But I have them. So many of them. Won't you do this? Please?"

"No."

"You are cruel."

"Refusing this childishness isn't cruel. It's practical. You're dead. And you're bored. Just wait and see if she finds your daughter for you. If you can move beyond this place, you'll forget all about your infatuation with dear Benedetta."

"So you say."

"So I know. Wait and see."

"I will never forgive you for this."

"Remind me to weep about that in a hundred years, if you're still here."

Chapter 17

Sigh Legends Of The Moon

Benny's hand in his was all that kept Dan on the ground. He'd never been much for whimsy. Today was an exception he hoped would become the norm. The sweet, slightly nutty, completely captivating woman beside him made all things possible, even making Daniel Greene the younger a man who could fly.

Weaving through the tombstones to the one marking his mother's grave, Dan's whimsy-balloon deflated just a little. Miranda Irene Greene once loved Tim, Charlie and Henny like sons. She'd have loved Benny by default, if for nothing else. He was certain she would have anyway. His mom loved everyone, and Benny was easy to love.

"I brought a cooler," he said as they settled on the blanket he spread on the ground. "Beer? Water?"

"Water. Thanks."

Dan handed her a bottle of water, cracked a beer for himself. Benny scooted between his legs, rested her back to his chest. They sat facing the tombstone, silent as his mother in her grave.

"She was only forty-one," Benny said softly. She tilted her head back, looked up at him. "That's just a year older than you are now. She was too young."

He took a bigger-than-necessary pull from his beer, swallowed the lump rising in his throat. "The cemetery is full of those who died too young."

Instead of stiffening as he feared, Benny snuggled more comfortably against him. "I don't think I knew she died this time of year. Is that why you watch the fireworks with her?"

I watch them with her now because I didn't when I should have. When I could have. Dan lifted the bottle to his lips, then set it down without drinking. "The accident was on the Fourth. Dad was drunk, as always.

Mom left me and Evelyn with our friends and took him home. They never got there. He died on impact. She hung on a few days."

Benny brought one of his hands to her lips, kissed it tenderly, lingered there. "I'm sorry, Dan. I didn't realize…there's only your mom's name on the stone. I thought…" She took a deep breath. "It must have been so hard, losing them both at once."

"It was hard losing Mom," he said. Above, the first stars twinkled to life. The pale pink and deep purple on the horizon would soon be gone, and the first rockets would blare into the sky. Dan gathered Benny closer. He buried his face in the hair at the nape of her neck. Love he never believed he'd feel for another living person soothed the rage, the grief this time of year always presented like an offering to old demons long quelled but never vanquished. He could tell Benny why his parents were not buried together, that he refused to subject her to an eternity with him for appearances never close to true. He could tell her he believed his mother crashed on purpose rather than continue on another day. He could tell her about abuse and depression and how badly parents could fuck up their kids' lives. But if he spoke the words, those demons so close to the surface this time of year would get loose, and Dan was not going to give them the satisfaction of ruining this day of days.

"When I was, oh, about eleven…" Benny spoke, her voice like a whisper out of the past. "I found a kitten out behind the post office. It was way too young to be separated from its mother. Cutest little thing. I was so afraid it would die. My dad is really allergic to cats. As it happens, so is Peter, but he wasn't born then. Anyway, I knew I couldn't keep it, but I couldn't put it back and hope someone else came by. I sat there crying for hours before someone noticed me and asked me what was wrong."

"You cried on a street corner in Bitterly, for hours, and no one stopped?"

"So I'm being dramatic." She laughed as softly as she spoke. "Let me finish my story."

"Okay. Sorry."

She smiled up at him. Above, the first rocket launched into the sky. "A man stopped. He said, 'Aren't you Timmy's baby sister?' And I think I told him I wasn't a baby. He asked what was wrong and I showed him the kitten. He took it from me and held it against him, to keep it warm, he said, because kittens so small couldn't regulate their own body temperature. He told me he'd take care of the kitten, if it was okay by me. His daughter had been asking for one. I thought he was the nicest man ever."

The hair on the back of Dan's neck prickled like a thousand ants skittering along his skin. Dan remembered the kitten. Evelyn had it until just before she and Paul moved to the renovated house on Division Street. "So what's your point? That my dad wasn't all bad?"

Benny sat on her knees, her arms winding about his neck. "I didn't know your father. Tim was scared of him, but I was just a kid. What would I have known? My point is that it's easier to remember the bad stuff, because we can be glad we don't have to deal with it with anymore. Remembering the good stuff is harder."

He never missed a daddy-daughter dance.

Dan closed his eyes, blocking out the fireworks sparkling and Benny's beautiful face. He rested his head to hers and tried. He tried so hard. But whatever good memory of Daniel Greene the elder might exist in his head, he couldn't bring it out.

"I'm sorry." Benny took his face in her hands. She kissed his nose, his cheeks, his lips. "Dan, I'm sorry. I was trying to help. I shouldn't have—"

"It's fine, Ben," he said, tried to grin and made it halfway to one. "It sucks to find out the funny-man is really the tragic clown, huh? What's that opera? Pagliacci?"

"I have no idea."

"And you call yourself Italian?"

"Don't joke."

Tears rolled down Benny's cheeks. He thumbed them away. "Better to laugh," he said. "My dad took too much from me, Benny. I'm not letting him have any more. I'm damn sure not giving him tonight."

"You can't bury these things."

"I don't bury them," he said. "I let them go. There's a huge difference. The past is the past, and unless you have some sort of time machine, there's no changing it."

"But—"

Dan kissed her silent.

"—you can be—"

He kissed her again, pulling her gently closer. Benny straddled his hips. She wound her arms about his neck, made no protest when he teased the t-shirt free of her jeans and slipped his hands underneath. Her body arched to his touch. She sighed against his lips. Overhead, a burst of light. A boom. Illuminating his mother's tombstone. His moment's pause gave Benny the chance to speak.

"You can be sad with me, Dan," she said. "Okay?"

"How could I ever be sad when you're around?" Rolling with her onto the blanket, his heart lurched. She squealed a half-hearted protest. Dan reached for the buttons of her jeans.

"Here?" Benny whispered. "On your mother's—"

Dan kissed her, swallowed the words he refused to hear. If he did, it would spoil everything, and he wasn't about to let it happen.

"She's not here." His fingers flicked open the top button, started on the second. "This is just a place for bones, Benny. Just their bones."

* * * *

You can do this, Benny. You can totally do this.

Leading Dan up the back stairs to her apartment, her hand in his, Benny gave herself the pep talk of her life. This was it. In moments, he would know they were having a baby. Would he weep? Whoop? Crack a joke? Whatever his reaction, Dan was going to be happy. Benny knew this beyond all doubt. The trembling of her insides wasn't fear, but the good kind of anticipation, akin to, if not the same as, the belly-churning sensation of making love to him in the cemetery. The goth-chick ever alive within her found it incredibly sexy even if it seemed a bit morbid to her adult self. At the time, she hadn't cared, and still didn't.

"I feel like a kid sneaking into your house when your parents aren't home." Dan kissed the back of her neck as she fumbled with the keys. She shoved him playfully off and opened the door.

"First of all," she said, "my parents will see your truck in the driveway when they get here. Secondly, my dad's going to grin like a Cheshire Cat and, thirdly, my mom will probably make us breakfast in bed, so…"

"Breakfast?" Dan waggled his pale eyebrows. "Is that an invitation to stay the night?"

"What did you think we were coming back here for?"

"Round two?"

"Daniel!"

"What? You think I can't?"

"I know you can." She tweaked the front of his jeans. "I'm counting on it."

She hung the keys on the hook beside the door, peeled off her hoodie and tossed it onto the couch. "Make yourself comfy. Want a glass of wine or something?"

"Sure, thanks." Dan flopped onto the couch, legs spread and arms across the back.

Benny closed her eyes and turned away before Henny's ghost superimposed itself in the exact position. The past was the past. There was no changing it.

"Red or white?" she called from the kitchen.

"Red's good."

Terri-Lynne DeFino

She uncorked the bottle of merlot waiting months for someone to drink it. Pouring, Benny squelched the image of Henny drinking from that glass, eating from that table, sleeping in that bed she hoped to take Dan to after she told him about Cricket. She poured herself lemonade. She sat beside him, a leg curled under her.

"You didn't have to open a bottle for me," he said. "I'd have had lemonade."

One of us needs to toast what I have to tell you with wine.

No, no, no. She needed something better.

That wine's been sitting on my counter since before you knocked me up.

Benny's cheeks burned. She pressed the cold glass to them.

"Dan, I have…I have something to tell you."

Dan set his wineglass down, took her lemonade from her and did the same. Turning sideways on the couch, he took her hands in his. "What's wrong? Tell me."

"Nothing's wrong. I just… I need to go to the bathroom."

Benny made a dash for the bathroom. Her head lightened and her lips buzzed. She sat on the toilet lid, head in her hands. "Dan has been here a million times," she told herself. "He's eaten at my table, watched football on my couch."

But he'd never slept in her bed. The bed she shared with Henny.

Benny slammed to her feet, looked herself squarely in the mirror. "Stop it," she growled. Softly. "Do you hear me? You just made love to him on his mother's grave and sleeping in the same bed with him here is bothering you? You're an idiot, Benedetta Marie Grady. You've already wasted too much time. You love him. He loves you. Now get out there and tell him you made a baby together."

She splashed water on her face, toweled off. Catching sight of her smug expression in the mirror, Benny chuckled softly, secretly. A loud bang cut it short. She cocked her head. "Dan? You okay out there?"

No answer. She flew out of the bathroom. "Dan?"

No Dan. Only an empty apartment. Outside, his truck sputtered to life. Benny flew to the door and onto the top landing in time to see him pull away, his tires spitting gravel.

"What the hell?"

Benny stumbled back into her apartment, looked stupidly around. Her lemonade sat dripping condensation onto her stained coffee table, but Dan's glass was gone. She found it in the kitchen. On the counter. Beside the ultrasound picture no longer pinned to her refrigerator door.

Chapter 18

Wildly Through The Woods

He didn't remember driving home. Dan only hoped he hadn't careened through the streets of Bitterly the way his thoughts were careening through his head. Flashed images of Benny, the fireworks, and the grainy image of what he knew to be an ultrasound picture danced like sparkles behind his eyes. His truck chewed gravel going up the driveway, stopped abruptly at the top. Dan slammed it into park, rested his head to the steering wheel, and tried to calm down.

A baby.

Was it his? Or had she not told him because it wasn't? Did he care? Maybe it was Henny's, a baby beyond the grave by way of sperm-kept-on-ice. It certainly wasn't a sibling. Peadar and Clarice Grady were way beyond their childbearing years. Peter's? A neighbor's? Anyone's besides Benny's? His better sense tried to reason with him, but irrational thoughts pushed them back.

Instead of bounding up the front steps, he headed to the entrance around back. Dan took the steps two at a time. The open door and bright lights showed Evelyn, at least, was home. He selfishly hoped the kids weren't. He needed to talk to his sister, to talk this out, to somehow make sense of the craziness whirring in his head. Passing through the kitchen, into the mudroom, he was stopped short by the voices coming from the family room beyond.

"…school where you'll go is really nice."

Paul's voice. Dan's stomach clenched.

"But what about my friends?" Mabel whined. "Daddy, can't you just move back here?"

"No," Evelyn said. "No, sweetie. We need a fresh start, away from Bitterly. You'll make new friends in Colorado."

"Can I learn how to snowboard?" Joss asked and Paul laughed—a sound Dan couldn't remember ever sounding real before. His scalp prickled, but he slipped quietly closer to the doorway, peered from the shadow of the mudroom, unseen. Paul sat on the floor, Joss between his legs and his arm around Mabel's shoulders. The man had changed, physically, at least. The marine-buzz haircut was now skater-dude shaggy. Gone was the power-suit and tie he once lived in and instead he wore jeans with holes in the knee, and some kind of graphic t-shirt.

"I'll teach you myself." Paul kissed his son's equally shaggy head. "I know it's a big change, and it feels like this is all coming out of nowhere, but your mom and I have been talking for a while…"

Dan backed slowly away, back into the kitchen, back outside. Betrayed. Twice in one night. By the only two women he loved, had loved, besides his mother. Ever. In the yard he built himself from stone to plant, Dan breathed deeply, slowly. Not even the Casablanca lilies' scent soothed. He tried to be happy for his sister, for his niece and nephew, and even for Paul. He really tried. Maybe if he hadn't found an ultrasound picture on Benny's refrigerator, he might have been.

Maybe if he had stuck around for an explanation.

There was no room for the small, rational voice inside his head. Seeing the picture on Benny's fridge had let loose those demons still too close for comfort. They dredged up the dazed, hurt, humiliated little boy on the ground, looking up at the man who had always been his hero. It gave him the teenager stepping between his parents, taking the smack that would have knocked his mother out, bearing the brunt of all his father's fury aimed at her for being whole and beautiful when he was ruined.

Dan needed to do something, something physical. Build a wall. Dig a hole. Mow a lawn. He slammed open the door of his detached garage, stood in the doorway looking for something, anything that would make him sweat. Not a project in sight. Dan was way too good at keeping up on things, and now it bit him in the ass.

And then he remembered.

He grabbed a shovel from the pegs. If Evelyn was moving to Colorado, this house would become his. He could do what he wanted, and right now, he wanted—needed—to sink that scrap of cement into the dirt under the grape arbor, put those kids' handprints where they belonged.

He struggled the heavy slab out of the garage. It fell on his toes once, twice. Dan gritted his teeth and struggled on. He slid it along the ground, scratching up the smooth concrete floor. Good. Something else to fix when he was done. He'd sink the slab and then mix up some patch.

He'd stay out all night fixing things until the demons were quiet and his thoughts tamed.

But Benny…she had to be thinking he was angry, for the way he'd blown out of her apartment.

Benny. Benedetta Marie Grady. The sound of her name inside his head echoed, shoved back at the past trying to bury him. Slumped against the garage wall, the slab of concrete resting against his legs, Dan wiped the sweat from his brow. He breathed in deeply. Exhaled long. It brought back more memories, this forced calm. Memories of the aftermath of black eyes and bruises. His mother's. His own. Dan vowed then he would fight his own impulse to lash out, to lose control. No matter how many times he wanted to punch his father back, Dan never did. Not once. He would not become what he hated most. Not then. And not now.

His racing heart slowed. The night's cool dried the sweat on his skin. Benny's name stopped echoing and instead whispered from his lips.

"Benny. A baby. My baby. Why didn't you tell me?"

Truth and calm and old vows upheld gave way to understanding. She had been about to tell him. As if she sat beside him speaking now, he heard her words. *Dan, I have something to tell you.* She'd been nervous, not afraid, and fighting her own pack of demons. Already those moments between getting up to refill his wineglass, seeing the picture stuck to the fridge and this moment, regaining his composure with a slab of concrete pressed up against his knees was blurring.

It had to have happened on Valentine's Day, until today, the only time they'd been together. He counted on his fingers. Almost five months. Dan's whole body shuddered. His baby was more than half-cooked. He'd already missed so much, but he would miss no more. Today was one of the best days of his life. Benny had invited him back to her apartment to tell him he was going to be a father, not to make love. Again. Though that would have happened too.

A door slammed inside the house. The lights were still on in the family room, but so too was the bathroom light upstairs. Joss. It had to be. He'd never met a door he wouldn't slam. Dan chuckled softly. It wouldn't be long before this house was silent, and his. Maybe Benny's too. He checked his watch. Would she be asleep? The weight of the way he bolted on her threatened, but Dan pressed back. It wasn't too late. He'd buy her flowers, beg her forgiveness, and she would give it.

But it was too late for flowers, even if he could find anything open on the Fourth of July. He stood up, brushing concrete dust from his jeans, and a better idea burst brilliant.

It would take longer than flowers, but Benny's happiness when she found out would be worth it. He hefted the slab and slid it carefully into the bed of his truck, fetched his shovel, and headed back toward town.

Chapter 19

Her Darker Moods

Benny knew better than to push. Pushing someone who wasn't ready to yield only resulted in getting pushed back. She had not anticipated Dan freaking out about the baby. Not one of the myriad of scenarios in her head had played out that way. But he had, and it did. Her absolute certainty about his expected happiness wavered through the night, and was obliterated by dawn.

She left before her parents were up, headed out to Savvy's first thing. Maybe she would accidentally-on-purpose run into Dan helping put the farm back together, but there was only Edgardo and Raul and the groggy high school students who worked Savvy's through the summer. Not even Savannah was there, and Benny remembered: though July 4th was the busiest day of the Bitterly year, July 5th was the one day her boss closed herself away from the world, unreachable as the moon and stars.

Edgardo and Raul shooed Benny off with words she didn't understand even if their meaning was clear. She got back onto her scooter, and headed for Division Street, telling herself she was just going to pass by and make sure he was safe at home.

Dan's truck wasn't in the driveway. Neither was it parked anywhere in town, or at Charlie and Johanna's out on County Line Road. As always when most in the need of comfort, she went to the cemetery.

Benny pulled up to the shade tree she always parked beneath, but she didn't get off her scooter. Closing her eyes and listening hard, she wished and wished and wished, but there was no answering whisper. No spectral fingers tickling down her back. No squeeze. Abandoned again. First Henny, then Augie, now Dan. The how didn't matter. In the end, Benny was just as alone.

A sob welled up from so deep inside, she almost felt as if she would vomit. For the first time in too many years, she wanted her mother.

Suddenly and acutely. She kicked the scooter back to life, and Benny did the unthinkable—she went the wrong way down the one-way cemetery road, zipped through the gates and barely stopped at the stop sign on the Green.

"Ma!" She raced up the steps and plunged into the kitchen, startling Clarice Grady from her coffee. "Oh, good. You're here. Let's go to Brooklyn today."

"Benny, my goodness." Clarice patted her chest. "What has gotten into you? Your scooter wasn't here this morning. I assumed you spent the night with…"

"No, I was here. I just left early to see if Savvy needed help. She doesn't, so I thought we could go into Brooklyn today instead of tomorrow. This way I won't have to take the day off work because I realized after the big picnic, Savvy would probably rather I not—"

"Benedetta, take a breath." Her mother cocked her head. "Did something go wrong with Daniel? You seemed absolutely giddy yesterday."

"I was. I am." Benny's laughter shook unconvincingly. "We had an amazing time together. I'm going to see him. Soon. He's busy today. I just want to go to Brooklyn, Ma. Can't we just go? You going to make me beg?"

A moment. Two that seemed an eternity. Benny's whole body trembled, and she hoped it was only on the inside.

"Of course we can, sweetheart. Give me half an hour to get dressed." Clarice pushed away from the table. She ran a hand along the tangle of Benny's hair, kissed her temple. "It's a good thing there are plenty of meatballs left for your father to eat today."

"Daddy can take care of himself," Benny mumbled.

"Oh, dear." Clarice Grady patted her daughter's head. "Whatever gave you that impression? I'll be down shortly. Have some breakfast while you wait."

Benny made toast and forced herself to eat it, and a cup of tea. True to her word, Clarice was ready and in the car within half an hour. She was not, however, in the driver's seat.

"What gives, Ma?"

"You drive." Her mother dangled the keys. "I'll take over when we get closer to the city. Brooklyn can be confusing, even for someone born and raised there."

"Then why don't you just drive?"

Clarice jiggled the keys. "Because it's time you drove further than the mall."

"I've driven further than the mall."

"When?"

Benny grimaced, grabbed the keys, and slid behind the wheel. Clarice made no more comment, but grinned in Benny's periphery, like a cat who got the cream.

* * * *

The drive was easy, mostly country highways designated scenic by all the travel guides. Switching from those rural highways to the interstates jittered Benny's belly. The trucks were so loud and careless drivers weaved in and out at speeds she had never driven. When had the speed limit gone up to sixty-five? Benny didn't give up the wheel when her mother suggested it, but she did opt for the cars-only-fifty-five-mph Saw Mill Parkway when given the chance.

After they stopped in a fast food place to get a soda and use the bathroom, Clarice took the wheel. "You did great, honey."

"Thanks," Benny said. "I should probably do things like this more often, huh?"

Clarice checked her mirrors. "You're waking up after a long sleep, Benny. Give yourself a break."

Tears threatened, but didn't fall. It was true. As her mother pulled into traffic, Benny thought back on the last six years of her life—her life after Henny. What did she remember about it? Until this past February, and Dan, not much. Since then, her life seemed a constant barrage of emotions and events whirring constantly in her head. Yes, she was waking up after too long a sleep. It was scary and sort of sad, but how exciting it was, too. She reached for her mother's hand, squeezed it gently. "Thanks for doing this with me today, Ma."

Clarice smiled. "My pleasure, sweetheart. I love spending time with you, and I'm happy to be going back to the old neighborhood, especially after losing the blue ribbon to Ginny Gordon. She's not even a little bit Italian. And did you taste those meatballs? Way too much oregano…"

Clarice chattered on about the big town picnic. Despite losing the blue ribbon, she'd had a marvelous time. Had Benny? She found herself telling her mother about the day spent with Dan, even about kissing on the Ferris wheel. Her mother knew just how to coax information out of her. She'd been doing it all of Benny's life. But it felt good. It felt familiar and loving. She kept imagining herself interjecting, "The food concessions were really spectacular this year. I especially loved the pulled pork. And, by the way, I'm having a baby in November and Dan's the father, but he freaked when he found out and now I have no idea what to do."

A dozen times, a dozen ways, but Benny couldn't manage to get out of her own head.

"The fireworks were a wonderful, weren't they?" Clarice asked.

Dan, the cemetery, the blanket and the boom that had little to do with pyrotechnics flashed through Benny's body, heating her from within. "They were amazing" she managed to say. "Really, really amazing."

"I didn't see you at the field."

"Dan and I watched from the cemetery. He does it every year."

"Oh, yes." Clarice sobered. "Of course he does, that darling boy."

"He's a man now, Ma."

Clarice smiled. "He will always be a boy to me, no matter how old he gets." And she sobered again. "It was a terrible day, that Fourth of July. One of the worst in my life. I let myself forget, after all these years."

"You and Daddy were pretty good friends with the Greenes, right?"

"Miranda was my very best friend," Clarice said, a catch in her voice. "We had the same middle name. We thought it was grand, and that it bound us in a special way. I loved her like a sister. It broke me when she died, for a long time."

"I don't remember you ever being broken."

"You were a teenager, and I covered it well."

"What about Mr. Greene?" Benny hedged. "Were he and Daddy friends?"

"They were, for a time." Clarice hesitated. "How much has Daniel told you about his parents?"

"That his dad was a drunk, and I got the idea he knocked Dan and his mother around."

"In the early days, Danny was a good man. He and Miranda were happy, like Daddy and me, and Charlie's parents and Henny's. We were all friends. Good friends. It was the Camelot of my life, back then, when we were all young and always together and our children were babies." Clarice sighed softly. "Danny fell off a roof when the boys were, oh, I believe they were four. Maybe five. I do know it was before kindergarten. He couldn't work. He started drinking. He turned mean. I wouldn't let Tim go play over there after a while, but Dan, your Dan, was always welcome in our home. It broke my heart, first time I saw Miranda with a black eye, and nearly killed me when I saw one on Dan."

"Why didn't you report him?"

"I'm ashamed of this answer," Clarice said, dabbing under her eyelashes with a tissue, "but back then, it's not something one did. If

Miranda would have left him, I'd have moved heaven and earth to help her. But she wouldn't. She just wouldn't."

"I'm sorry, Ma. I didn't mean to make you cry."

"Oh, Benny, I cry about Miranda now and then without your help. I will tell you a secret if you promise not to get angry with me."

"How can I promise when I have no idea what you're about to say? I'll try. How's that?"

"Good enough." Clarice gripped the wheel with both hands, checked her rearview, changed lanes. "I always hoped you'd end up with Daniel, Benny. I loved Henny like my own son. I did and I will always wish things happened differently. But Daniel is special to me, because his mother was my very best friend, and I couldn't help her, and she died. But also because he's one of the best people I know. He is a good man, Benny. The kind every mother hopes her daughter will marry."

"Marry?" Benny choked. "Isn't that presuming a bit much?"

"Maybe." Clarice shrugged. "A mother can hope, can't she? Are you angry?"

Benny slumped back in her seat. "Nah," she said. "You and Daddy loved Henny, no doubt about that. Besides, if I'm angry with you for loving Dan too, then what do I do with myself?"

"Then...you do love him?"

Benny let go a long sigh. "I'm afraid so."

"Then why so forlorn?

She almost said it. She came the closest she had in the whole two hours they'd been in the car. Benny even opened her mouth, the words on the tip of her tongue and ready to fly out, but she said, "I just have some more stuff to work out before I actually tell him."

Clarice, thankfully, let it go with a nod and a smile.

Chapter 20

She Crowds With Ghosts

It was the Sunday after the Fourth. In Brooklyn. The streets were fairly quiet. "Everyone's at the beach," her mother said as she parked the car. "Did you check to see if On the Fire is even open today? I can't tell. The awning is shading the window."

Benny hadn't. Not until they got as far as the Kosciuszko Bridge, and then she had done a quick and clandestine internet search.

"Yes, of course I checked. It's open noon until six o'clock."

"This is so exciting." Clarice gathered her purse. "I hope it's still good. Oh, wouldn't it be a shame if it went downhill? I still can't wait to eat something."

Benny ducked out of the car and waited for her mother on the sidewalk. She kissed her cheek. "Meatballs, perhaps?"

"No, thank you. I don't want to see another meatball for at least a month."

Quiet as were the streets, On the Fire was packed, and only after walking in and waiting for a hostess did Benny realize it was full of family, not customers.

"Oh, I'm sorry," she said to the hostess searching for an empty spot at the table. "The internet said you were open today."

"We are," the young lady told her. "We've just got a lot of family in for the holiday weekend. Hang on a sec. I'll clear a space down at the end. You want to be next to one another, or across?"

"It doesn't matter. Whatever you have."

The hostess winked and left them.

"I'm going to use the ladies room," Clarice whispered "I'll be right back."

Benny stood in the cool, taking it all in. Photos lined the dark, wood-paneled walls. Friends. Family. A whole lot of celebrities caught enjoying a meal and wine. Photos dating all the way back to the 1950s. Though there were a few tables-for-two along the wall, long tables dominated the floor, like a banquet or a wedding. The hostess was even now clearing a spot near the end of one of those tables still full of the large and obvious family already there.

If she had wondered how On the Fire lasted so long when so many eateries didn't last five years, Benny no longer did. A meal here wasn't just a night out, it was an event. It was a party. It was a good time with good people over good food. The scent of garlic and onions, basil and roasting meat didn't just linger in the air. It permeated the walls, the curtains, the chairs and tables and floor. The aroma from decades of good food, hours of happiness, and thousands of conversation were ghosts unable to depart. Benny felt them as intimately as she did Augie before she accidently looked at him.

Her eyes were drawn to the portrait of an extraordinarily beautiful woman hanging on the back wall, her smooth cheek pressed to an old man's lined one. Flora Fiore, or whatever her name had become after Augie's supposed death. Benny glanced over the faces populating the place, both in the flesh and on the walls. Whether real or wistful thinking, she saw Flora's nose here, her thick, curly hair there, the plump bow of her mouth everywhere. When the young hostess turned back to wave them to the table, Benny saw the thick, dark eyelashes of the woman in the portrait.

"You look like her." Benny pointed to the portrait. "Is she a relative?"

"Nona Florina?" She smiled over her shoulder. "She was my great-grandmother. And thank you. She was ridiculously gorgeous."

Benny's heart fluttered. Augie's great-great-granddaughter. So close she could throw her arms around her and hug her tight.

"You said was," Benny said. "Does that mean she's…departed?"

"Yeah, sadly. She'd have been ninety this year. Why? Did you know her?"

"Sort of. My mother grew up in this area. She remembers this place well. And…" How much should she say? If Flora would have been ninety, telling this girl she was friendly with her great-grandmother's natural father was going to sound ridiculous. "It's kind of complicated. I heard a sad story about a man who lived in my town, and as it happens, it's about a woman, your Nona Florina, I think, who lived here where my mother grew up. I thought it was kind of kismet, so I dragged my mother back to the old digs to see if there was anything I could do to put an end to the story. Or at least appease my curiosity."

"Kismet?"

"Fate?" Benny tried.

The girl nodded. "Oh, sorry. I'm Raquel, by the way. And you are?"

"Benedetta Grady," Benny said. "But my mother's maiden name was Cioffi."

"Hey, Uncle Tony," Raquel shouted over the noise behind her. "You know the name Cioffi?"

A big man about Clarice's age stood up from the table, squinted their way. "Who's asking?"

"This lady here says her mom's a Cioffi and she used to—"

"Tony Pagano, is that you?" Clarice stood in front of the ladies' room door, a hand to her chest and her mouth a perfect O.

Tony turned her way, his arms opened up. "Clara Cioffi, where the fuck've you been, ah?"

Benny was pulled in along with her mother, paesan' returning home to Brooklyn. They were passed from person to person, introduced, kissed and hugged. They were coaxed into chairs and handed plates overflowing with fried calamari, eggplant rollatini, fried zucchini blossoms and, the house special since the doors first opened, braised rabbit. Benny felt as if she'd been thrown back in time. The only thing missing was one of those famous old crooners singing from the radio. As if out of her thoughts, someone changed the station from whatever soft jazz had been playing to the Sinatra satellite station.

...be where little cable cars climb halfway to the stars
The morning fog may chill the air, I don't care...

"My love waits there," Tony Pagano belted out along with the radio, his voice a surprising tenor. "Above the blue and windy sea..."

"When I come home to you, San Francisco," everyone but Benny joined in. "Your golden sun will shine for me!"

"Oh, goodness," Clarice—Clara to those in the restaurant—said breathlessly. "I was so in love with Tony Bennett as a girl. I named my only daughter after him."

"Ma! Does Daddy know?"

"Of course not. So don't you go telling him." Clarice threw back her head and laughed, her cheeks flushed and her eyes bright.

Tony put an arm around the back of her chair as it started to wobble, and his wife slapped playfully at his arm. Benny imagined her mother as a much younger woman, sitting in this very restaurant with these same people, a complete stranger. She had always known that Clarice Cioffi left Brooklyn for college, met the man she would marry and didn't go back, but she never imagined her making jokes and laughing too loud, singing along with the radio.

This is who she was. Benny's eyes strayed to Tony Pagano's wife. That is who she would have been.

"You guys sure picked the right day to come," Raquel said, leaning over Benny's shoulder. "I don't think my uncle is going to let her leave."

Benny checked her watch. It was already after two, they had a nearly three-hour drive ahead of them, and she had found out nothing about Flora other than she was this girl's great-grandmother.

"This is going to sound strange," she said to Raquel, "but is there someone I can talk to about your Nona Florina."

"Oh, yeah. Right." Raquel straightened. "Ma!"

A woman Benny thought had been introduced as Tina looked their way. Benny hushed Raquel as inconspicuously as possible.

"It's okay. I'll go talk to her myself, thanks." Benny headed toward Raquel's mother, hand extended. "Tina, right?"

"Yeah, Christina, but everyone calls me Tina."

Benny sat in the empty chair beside her. "You own this place?"

"Sort of. On the Fire has always been family run and owned, but I'm in charge, if that's what you're asking."

"Actually, I wanted to talk about Flora."

"My grandmother?"

Benny's gaze flicked quickly to a pair of women obviously listening. She turned her back, lowered her voice. "This is going to sound a little strange, but someone who loved her very much lived in Bitterly, the town where I am from, and he—"

"Bitterly, Connecticut?"

"You're familiar with it?"

"I know of it."

Tina said no more for a long moment, instead looking carefully at Benny through narrowed eyes. Beautiful eyes, but not Flora's.

"It's not me you want to talk to," Tina said at last. "You want my mother."

"One of Flora's daughters?"

Tina nodded. "She's not here, though. She doesn't come out much since Pop died."

"Oh, I'm sorry."

"You know how these old Italians are. Pop's been gone ten years and she's still wearing black. Only time she goes out is for another funeral."

"You sure she'll talk to me?"

"About Nona Florina?" Tina grinned. "Oh, she'll talk. If there's one thing old Italians like better than a funeral, it's talking about the dead. Saints, every one of them. But in Nona's case, it's true. Come with me."

Benny followed Tina to a hallway in the back of the restaurant and, after looking once over her shoulder, followed her into it. At the end was a staircase leading up, to a surprisingly big and airy apartment that smelled as garlicky-good as it did downstairs. The spotless furniture came straight out of the fifties. The couch in the parlor was covered in plastic, as were the two wingback chairs. Above the ancient fireplace hung a ceramic relief of The Last Supper. On the mantel, figurines of the Virgin Mary and Saint Francis of Assisi perched among the tchotchke from New York City, Venice, and Rome.

On every creamy-white wall hung a crucifix. On every flat surface was a silk flower arrangement sitting atop a doily crocheted by some long-deceased relative, Benny was certain. In the arched opening separating the living space from the bedrooms, Tina told her to wait while she knocked on a closed door.

"Mama?" Tina's voice was softer than it had been downstairs. "You sleeping?"

"In the middle of the day?" came the quick response, but slumber trembled the high, frail voice. "What is it, dear? Everything all right downstairs?"

"Everything's fine. I brought someone to see you."

"Oh, I'm not presentable for company."

"Mama, don't be silly. It's just an old friend of a friend."

Tina went into the room and closed the door behind her. Muffled voices and what sounded like the news on the television or radio came through the wall. While she waited, Benny studied the dozens of framed photos on the wall. Kids' school pictures spanning the decades from the black-and-white sixties through the photo-shopped, neon backgrounds of the present. Wedding photos, graduation photos, baby's first Christmas-Easter-Halloween photos. Benny tried to match the young faces to the older ones. Familial traits became obvious—the hook of a nose, the exotic eyes and lashes like thick smudges of coal. She wondered which of those traits belonged to Augie, and then wondered how he was able to write off this whole piece of what should have been his life.

He didn't. *That's why he's stuck.*

"Benedetta?" Tina's head appeared around the doorjamb. "Her highness is ready to see you now."

"Christina Marie!"

Tina winked.

Benny smiled. "We share a middle name."

"Yeah, the two of us and about ninety percent of all Italian girls." Tina gestured her back into the parlor. "Even Nona Florina's middle name was Maria."

Benny sat on the couch that squeaked when she did so. Tina rolled her eyes and they shared an unspoken joke, softly, so the tiny woman breezing into the room didn't hear them. She was as frozen in the 1970s as her home was in the 1950s. The jet-black, old-lady-helmet-short hair, penciled-in eyebrows and lipstick the color of bubblegum made her a dolled-up version of Edith Bunker, right down to the sensible shoes and nylons, the starched apron over her knee-length, black dress. She had none of Flora's visible grace and beauty, though she had certainly passed on the genes to her granddaughter, Raquel. When she lowered herself daintily to the wingback chair—that also squeaked—she perched on the edge like a bird poised and ready to fly off.

"Mama, this is Benedetta Grady. Benedetta, this is my mother, Mrs. Iapaluccio."

"You may call me Carmen," she said.

"And please, call me Benny."

Carmen inclined her head. "Who are your people, Benny?"

"My people?"

"I told her your mother used to live here in Bensonhurst. She's asking your family name."

"Oh, Cioffi," Benny answered, and Carmen's cheeks pinked.

"I remember the family well. Good people. I don't think there are any left in the neighborhood anymore."

"I don't think so either."

"Well then." Carmen smoothed her apron. "Christina tells me you knew someone who loved my mother? Someone from your home town?"

"I do, kind of. It's a bit complicated…" Benny stuck to the truth as much as possible, leaving the implausible out completely. Those things she had learned of Augie and his daughter left behind in Italy, she said she read in some old letters her friend, who lived in the house Augie built for his second family, found in the cellar during renovations. Tina and Carmen exchanged glances, but neither interrupted her.

"So here I am in Brooklyn," she said, "hoping to put this story to rest. From what I've learned, he died without ever telling Flora who he was, without ever fulfilling his promise to her. I hoped his daughter was still living, and that I could tell her about her father, and how sorry he was, maybe put his spirit to rest."

"You think it is restless?" Carmen asked.

"I do, yes." Benny looked her straight in the eyes. "It sounds a little nuts-o, but when I visit his grave, I feel it. He was afraid to put this to rights in life. It weighed on him before his death. I can only imagine it continued after."

Carmen looked at her, head cocked and eyes wide. "You are sensitive to such things. I can tell."

"Mama, come on. Don't start."

"You hush. I may not have inherited my mother's great beauty, but I did inherit her sensitivity. I perceive things others don't." She leaned closer to Benny. "You understand what I mean, don't you, dear?"

Tina blew out an exaggerated breath.

Benny nodded.

Carmen continued looking at her, a gentle smile playing at her lips. "Would you fetch Nona Florina's album for me, Tina? It's in my chest, down in the cellar."

"Sure, Mama." She groaned as she stood up, the couch squeaking along with her. "Don't creep Benny out while I'm gone."

Benny fidgeted. The couch squeaked and she stilled. The uneasy sensation of being out of a loop she should know all about raised the hair on her arms. Carmen reached over and patted her knee.

"You look like you just swallowed a bug, dear."

"I do? Oh. Sorry."

Carmen's laughter sounded like fluttering bird wings. "I can see it in you. But I can also see you hold it in check. It's all right dear." She stopped Benny's protest with a tiny, raised hand. "Some of us are content to simply accept they are there."

It was on the tip of Benny's tongue to tell this sweet, strange woman the truth behind her visit, but it would take far too long, and she was not entirely certain Carmen, who was looking beyond her rather than at her, actually had all her marbles.

"He is a naughty one," she said, and giggled like a girl.

"Pardon?"

"He was hiding behind a big tree, and he jumped out at you. When you screamed, he pulled you into his arms and kissed you. You were both so young."

Benny's face burned. Her belly churned, and for the first time all day, she thought about Henny. And Dan.

"That was the first time Henny, my late husband, kissed me," Benny said. "How did you know?"

"He showed me."

"What do you mean he showed you?"

"I wish I could explain it, dear. I can't."

Bile rose to Benny's mouth. She smacked her lips, tried to swallow it down. "May I have a glass of water?"

"Of course, dear." Carmen flittered into the kitchen.

Benny pressed her palms to her cheeks. How could she discredit the old woman's words when she herself was in Brooklyn at the bequest of a man dead more than thirty years?

"Here you go." Carmen handed her a glass. "Nice and cool, but not too cold. I squeezed a little lemon into it for you, too."

"Thank you."

"I didn't mean to upset you."

"You didn't."

"I did. Forgive me. I don't usually pass messages along. Most don't receive them well, or they look at me like I'm a crazy old lady. They forget I wasn't always old. But you are different, Benny, and he is just so charming. Oh!" Carmen's paled. She patted her face with the tips of her fingers. "Oh, my."

"What is it? Tell me. Please."

"He...he shows me trees, sunshine, a road, and...I feel the engine underneath me. The wheels. The sunlight and the road. And..." Her bright eyes found Benny's. "I am so sorry, Benedetta."

Benny was crying now, softly and without sound. "It's okay."

"He wants you to know...to know..." A silent moment, then a slow smile formed on bubblegum pink lips. "He says he didn't crash, not where he is. He rode out of this life and onto another road that goes on and on and on. He wants to see where it leads, if it's all right with you."

"I would never hold him back."

"But you do, Benedetta. And only you can release him."

"Then I release him."

"Not with words, dear. Not with—" Tina's footsteps coming back up the stairs startled the old woman silent. "Don't tattle on me," she whispered. "Tina didn't inherit my mother's beauty or her perception. She's all her pig-headed father, rest his soul."

Benny nodded, finished the water in her glass, breathed slowly and deeply until her heart stopped trying to jump out of her chest. By the time

Tina trudged into the room carrying the old photo album, she was mostly in control.

"I hope this is the right one," Tina said, "because I am not going back down there. When's the last time anyone dusted? Or even looked at anything in the cellar? I swear, if I looked hard enough, I'd find old Aunt Paulina rattling around down there."

"Aunt Paulina died back in the eighties, honey."

"My point exactly."

Carmen held out her hands for the photo album, a heavy thing with hard covers and black pages, and photos held in place with tiny triangular tabs. She flipped to the first page.

"Yes, this is the one." She motioned Benny in, turning the album her way, and pointing to the toddler standing between a pair of somber-looking adults. "This little angel is my mother, Flora. This is her mother, Carmen, and this is her father—"

"Augie…" Every other thought left Benny's head. She slid the photo album from Carmen's lap to her own. The mother was indeed quite beautiful, but the child in the photo and the woman on the wall downstairs looked just like her father.

"There is a better one of him, on the next page." Carmen tapped the album.

Benny turned the page, and gasped. Handsome didn't even begin to cut it. Augie was a lady-killer from the waves of black hair to the sparkle in his light eyes. Blue, she imagined. Startling, because they would be like ice, yet somehow warm as sunshine. This was no somber image taken in the Old Country. By his clothes and the picture quality, Benny guessed it was taken in the 1950s, and in the restaurant downstairs at that. Its placement in the album told her much more. "She knew it was him, didn't she."

"She did," Carmen said. "She brought the first photo with her when she came to America. It was one of her only possessions, and her most prized. The second one was taken by the man who raised her—Papasandro, we all called him. No sweeter man has ever lived. He recognized Flora's natural father when he first came through the door."

They had lived in the same small village in Campania, though Alessandro—Papasandro—had been much older. When he learned the infamously beautiful Carmen Fiore had been widowed and left to raise a little girl on her own, he courted and won her heart, despite the vast difference in their ages. Family stories passed down through the years said their marriage was a happy one right up until the war separated them. Flora was sent to live with relatives in America, Sandro was put to work for the army, and Carmen died without ever seeing her husband or daughter again.

"Papasandro didn't know his wife lied to him about her first husband's death," Carmen said. "It wasn't until the supposedly dead man walked through the door of the restaurant that he suspected the man had actually abandoned his wife and child. He wanted to be certain it was him, so he took the picture of their new friend to compare it to the one in the album. As you can see, there is no doubt."

Older, yes, but unmistakably the same man. Benny took a deep, shuddering breath. "No, no doubt whatsoever. He was very handsome."

"He was." Carmen ran a finger lovingly over his photo. "Charming too. And kind. I don't remember much about him, but he used to bring me, my sister and brother sweets whenever he came in to eat. He'd sneak them to us like it was some great secret."

"And Papasandro?" Benny asked. "Did he tell Flora who Augie— August was?"

"At first, I am certain he was quite angry, but my grandfather didn't have it in him to sustain such a thing. I can't be certain, but I believe he might have come to feel sorry for August, having given up such a treasure as his beloved Florina, but Papasandro's loyalty was to her. He took his secret to the grave, to shield her from the truth that her father had not died, but chosen to disappear."

"And that's where it gets Shakespearean," Tina drawled. "Papasandro was protecting her, and she was protecting him."

Benny's scalp prickled. "She already knew?"

"She did," Carmen answered. "I am named for my grandmother. By all accounts, a harder woman has never lived, but she loved her child. My mother always told me that my grandmother never spoke badly of Augusto, but honored him as any woman would honor her dead husband. She is the one who gave my mother the first photo, before putting her on the ship bound for America. Like Papasandro, Flora recognized her father the moment he walked in."

"And she never confronted him?"

"It wasn't her way."

"But wasn't she angry? Or sad? For all she knew, her father abandoned her." Benny swallowed hard, but failed to swallow the truth. "Even in the best case scenario, he did abandon her. He let his wife's lie stand, even after finding her again."

"Oh, dear, I can't say what her secret thoughts and sorrows were," Carmen said. "I can only tell you my mother was an extraordinary woman, Benny. She loved. Everyone and everything got the benefit of the doubt, and most had no choice but to live up to her faith in them. She told the story of her life without shame or grief. I have always known she had a papa who raised her, and one who fathered her. She loved them both for what they gave to her."

"She told me," Tina added, "she believed August loved her very much. He used to come to the restaurant, and she would catch him looking at her with such love in his eyes. After a while, she figured there was a reason he kept quiet, and she respected it. Love doesn't always have to be shouted, she said. Sometimes, it could just be."

Just be. The words echoed ear to ear. Benny let them fade.

"Augie regrets...regretted what he did, but he did love Flora very much. By what I learned, he was afraid of losing his wife and children and his place in the world. It sounds so terrible," Benny confessed, "so selfish."

"Those were different times." Carmen tsked. "Propriety would have made things very difficult for everyone involved. My mother was a happy woman, Benny, and it was because she would not hold onto the anger and grief she had every right to. If not for the lie her mother told, she wouldn't have been raised by Papasandro, and she loved him at least as much as he loved her. If not for Papasandro, she probably would have died in the war with her mother and grandmothers. Because he sent her to America, she met her husband, my father. A better man has never lived, and he adored her too. Without him, she would not have had her children, or opened the restaurant that has brought us all prosperity and happiness. There is no room for regret in a life well lived. It's what she always told me, and what I believe I have passed on to my children."

"You do?"

"Christina Marie!"

"I'm just kidding, Mama." Tina kissed her mother's cheek, then turned to Benny. "I'm different," she said. "I loved my Nona Florina, but I never understood how she was able to just let stuff go. No matter who wronged her. No matter what she lost. 'Eez okay,' was her favorite thing to say, and when she said it"—Tina shrugged—"it was."

"What good is holding it tight?" Carmen asked. "Would it have changed anything?"

"Maybe not." Tina grinned. "But we Italians are wired for vengeance."

"Not all of us, dear."

"Well, I am. If I found out you had a husband before Daddy, and he abandoned me to live another life, I'd hunt him down and gut him."

Carmen leaned toward Benny, whispering dramatically, "See? She is all her father, just like I told you."

"Is that so bad?" Tina asked.

"You are the perfect you, Christina. I wouldn't have you any other way." The old woman rose to her feet, signaling the discussion was at an end. Benny and Tina followed suit.

"If you would put the album away for me, honey," Carmen said, "Benny can help me bring the cannoli downstairs."

"You made cannoli?"

"Of course I did. It is not a family gathering without my cannoli."

"I can send one of the kids up."

"No need. Benedetta's here. You don't mind, do you, dear?"

"Not at all."

Tina gathered up the album. "You're up to something, Mama."

"Me? What can I possibly be up to? Benny, ignore her and come with me to the kitchen."

Carmen started for the kitchen, Benny on her heels. When the door to her apartment whispered open and clicked closed, the old woman, paused in her steps, but only a moment, and moved to the refrigerator.

"He was my grandfather. August was." She opened the refrigerator door. "My biological grandfather, and the man responsible for so many of those downstairs, but I know almost nothing about him. Can you share anything with me?"

"Oh, of course." Benny took the tray of cannoli and set them down on the counter indicated. The shells were the perfect gold, dusted with powdered sugar. It took all her willpower not to stick her finger—accidentally, of course—into the smooth and decadent ricotta-cream filling. Benny's mouth watered just a little. "Well, he had a wife named Katherine, and three children—Philip, Victor, and Adrianna. He was a builder, and lived in Bitterly from about 1935 until he died in 1980. My friend lives in the house he built—"

"The friend who found the letters that brought you here."

"Y-yes." Benny cleared her throat. "In the cellar."

Carmen only nodded and retrieved another tray. When she handed it to Benny, her pink lips pursed as if she were trying not to smile, and did not let go. Cold heat rushed to Benny's face. She stammered words she didn't recognize, sounds that didn't even seem quite human. The more uncomfortable she got, the more pursed became Carmen's lips, until she burst out laughing. "There were no letters, were there, Benedetta."

"No." The word came out in a rush of breath. "I…he…it's just he…"

"You need not explain, dear. Least of all to me. It is a kind thing you do. That's all that matters."

Benny threw what little caution she had left—along with all sense and reason—to the wind. "He can't move on," she confessed. "He is stuck between here and there, because he made a promise to his daughter he didn't keep. I don't know how to help him, even now."

"August is going to have to help himself," Carmen said. "There is no ill-will toward him by those he left behind. He is not held, but holding. But perhaps…" She paused, a finger tapping at her chin. "Yes, that might help."

"What?"

"Wait here." Carmen led her back to the parlor and left her there. She returned a moment later with a wooden box the size of a cigarette case. "Come with me."

Instead of going to the stairs Tina brought her up by, the old woman led her to a covered staircase zigzagging down two stories to the back yard. Once again Benny was surprised by the size of it, and the grace. It wasn't the sweeping lawn and gardens of Bitterly, but there was a concrete patio, a grape arbor burgeoning with green leaves, and a vegetable patch of neat rows. Eggplant, tomatoes, peppers, zucchini, herbs and herbs and herbs. It was to this patch Carmen led her, letting go of Benny and scooping a tiny handful of dirt from it.

"My mother grew all the vegetables and herbs she used in the restaurant, right in this very same patch," she said. "On the Fire was half the size then. Now, this is mostly for the family. Here, take this and open it."

She handed Benny the wooden box. The faded picture on the lid had once been of a buxom, black-haired woman dressed in slinky red. Black letters rubbed mostly to the wood spelled out—*Escarlata*. All four sides showed the words *Cigarros Cubanos*. Benny flipped the tiny brass catch and opened the box.

"Soil from Italy," Carmen told her. "Mama brought it with her when she came to America. She didn't want to leave her home, her mother. Nona Carmen filled this box so she would always have a little bit of home wherever she went."

"Did she ever go back to Italy?"

"Sadly, no. The restaurant didn't allow for vacations, even when there was enough money for one. I remember, she used to take the box out every once in a while and just smell it." Carmen tipped the American soil from her hand into the Italian soil, re-latched the lid and closed Benny's hand on the old cigar box. "Take it to him," she said. "Tell him Flora knew him, and she loved him. See if it helps."

Benny looked at the box in her hand, mouth agape and eyes staring. She held something sacred in her hand—a gift of love, a piece of home. Solace in sad times and comfort a life long. She held the history of the Cuban cigars smoked, maybe by Augie himself, and soil tended when the world was still at peace. Soil from a New World garden that fed the same family all their lives. Now she would bring it to Augie. She would close the circle left open too long. Maybe, indeed, it would help.

"Thank you, Carmen." She kissed the old woman's soft cheek. "You are your mother's daughter. I can tell."

"The highest compliment I can ever hope for. Thank you, Benedetta. I barely knew him, but I always loved him. I hope he finds peace. And, perhaps, if you wouldn't mind, pass his story along to the children he had with Katherine, if they still live. They have family they never knew existed, and so do we. If they have any interest, they can contact me here."

"I will find them," Benny promised. "There has to be some record in town. My mom has spent decades doing our family genealogy. She knows how to find people."

"That would be lovely. Now then"—Carmen took her arm—"be a good girl and go fetch those cannoli I promised Tina before she goes looking for them herself. Bulldog of a woman, she is. Just like her father, rest his soul."

Chapter 21

The Wind's Dim Words

Benny drove home. All the way. Aside from some traffic again on Kosciuszko Bridge, she did okay. Summer was high and sunlight lingered long. By the time she reached the rural highways closer to home, the sky was still evening-pink.

Clarice—no longer Clara—Grady mostly dozed while the radio played softly. Benny was content to let her bask in the old memories lingering along with the sunshine, grateful her mother had been satisfied with, "Oh, right. Sadly, she died years ago," after she asked Benny about the old man's daughter they went all the way to Brooklyn to find.

"Too bad," she'd said. "Oh, that's a shame. But we had a good day, didn't we honey?"

"A really good day, Ma."

Clarice had already promised her old friends she would return in September for the Feast of San Gennaro. Benny would be recruited, along with her father and Peter, and couldn't be happier to oblige.

"Stop at Teddy's," her mother's dreamy voice said. "I want to get your father one of those toffee bars he loves so much. I don't get down here much."

"Oh, so you still remember him then?" Benny teased. "I thought Tony Pagano might have swept him right out of your mind."

Clarice smiled without opening her eyes. "Tony'd have grown out his hair and worn a dress if I asked him to, back in the day," she said. "Handsome as he was, I didn't want to marry an Italian man."

"Really? Why?"

"Maybe I should say, I didn't want to marry any Italian man of my acquaintance." Clarice picked up her head. "I wanted an educated man, someone not so set on tradition."

"And you married Daddy?"

"Oh, goodness, Benny. Where do you think you get your rebellious nature from? Me? Your father was as close to an anarchist as anyone I've ever known. He's mellowed, but he was a wild one, my Peadar, always stirring up trouble, handing out pamphlets and flyers. He was so blonde, back then, like Timmy was, remember? There were no boys like him back home in Brooklyn. Still, we dated, but I wouldn't get serious about him, no matter how I felt. Not for a long time."

"Why not?"

"I was always well aware of how lucky I was, Benny. Brooklyn may be New York City, but there were, and still are, pockets that seem to exist twenty years behind the times. I lived in one of them. A young woman going to college wasn't exactly the norm. I didn't want to go from high school to engaged to married and pregnant all before the age of twenty."

"Ma, you married Daddy right after college."

"Not right after. I was twenty-four, and had been out on my own for two full years before I finally agreed to marry him. He'd been asking for years, my poor man. It seems close to traditional, from your standpoint. But from mine, it was a huge step out of what was, and into a bigger world. There's Teddy's." Clarice pointed. "I'll just be a minute."

Her mother hurried into the roadside shop, no longer the same Ma Benny had always known. Until today, Clarice Irene Grady had always been, in her daughter's eyes, a housewife and mother too wrapped up in her children's lives to have one of her own. But she'd been a young woman living in Brooklyn once, in New York City. She went to college and got her degree in history. She worked and lived on her own for two years, and Benny had no idea where she'd done either.

"I bought half-a-dozen." Clarice returned with a little bag, already blooming butter. "It's a nice treat for all of us, unless Daddy sees them before I set them out for dessert."

Benny put the car in gear and pulled back onto the road. "Speaking of Daddy, I was just wondering something."

"What's that, honey?"

"You said he waited a long time for you to agree to marry him."

"Five years in all."

"And you worked and lived on your own for two years after college."

"I did." Clarice's laughter seemed slightly forced. "Where is this going?"

"I have no idea what your job was. Or his, for that matter."

"I worked for the Museum of Natural History in New York," her mother answered in a breath exhaled. "In the archives. The pay was terrible, and

I only got the job because my father knew someone who knew someone, but it was very prestigious. At least, I thought so."

"And Daddy?"

"He was a freelance photographer. He worked the department stores taking portraits, and pictures with Santa during the holidays. He made enough doing that to allow what he really loved, doing piecemeal work for the local papers for the most part."

"Daddy lived in the City?"

"We did, for those two years. I loved it. Those were exciting times."

"Why'd you move up to Connecticut, then?"

"Because your father was convinced I wouldn't marry him because he had no steady job. He wanted to be a photojournalist so badly, but he got a job with a big real estate firm taking pictures of houses in Stamford and presented me with this ring." She held out her hand, the tiny diamond there all the years of Benny's life sparkling in the day's last light. "How could a woman refuse after a sacrifice like that?"

"His wasn't the only sacrifice. You had to give up your apartment in New York."

"Yes, well…" Cheeks were definitely a shade too pink, Clarice fidgeted. "Our…my apartment was on the shabby side, so…"

"Ma?" she asked, trying not to smile. "Where did Daddy live during those two years?"

"Where did he live? I thought I already told you. In New—"

"—York. Yes, I got that part. But where? In proximity to you, I mean."

"In proximity to me?" She checked her lipstick in the visor mirror, opened and closed her window. Finally, she said, "We lived together, Benedetta Marie, and you'd already guessed, so I don't see the reason for torturing me."

"You could have just said it."

"It was the seventies. And I told you, your father was an anarchist."

"You don't have to defend it to me. What did your twenty-years-behind-the-times family have to say about it?"

Clarice bit her lip. "We hid it from them. And it wasn't easy when they insisted on dropping by to surprise me all the time, I'll tell you."

"And you claim Daddy was the rebel."

"It was the seventies. Everyone was a rebel back then."

It wasn't true, and Benny knew it. Even when she was a kid watching re-runs of *Three's Company*, unmarried couples cohabitating was still taboo.

"You had a whole life I've always been clueless about," Benny said. "How is that possible?"

"Children think their parents will only ever see them as children, and it is kind of true," Clarice answered. "But kids are way worse when it comes to seeing their parents as actual people. I'm your mother, the woman who baked cupcakes on your birthday, and went to PTA meetings, and had sex only the three times it took to conceive you and your brothers."

"Ew, Ma."

"See? You know what you want to, and let the rest go."

"I would prefer to stay blissfully ignorant of your sex life, but I do like knowing about your life before Bitterly. And I liked when you told me about Miranda."

"I liked telling you," Clarice said. "I should have done it when you were younger, so you wouldn't have to feel the need to keep things from me. We are women, Benny. Mother and daughter, yes, but not mother and child. I think it's time we saw one another as adults, who can share things about their lives instead of shield one another from them, don't you?"

The hair on the back of Benny's neck prickled. That cold heat of knowing what she should have all along rushed through her. Pulling the car over to the side of the road, Benny put the hazards on. Hands gripping the wheel and eyes straight ahead, she said, "You know about the baby, don't you."

Clarice took Benny's hand from the steering wheel, kissed it. "Of course I do, honey."

"Since?"

"Oh, since around April when I realized you hadn't been coming around to whine about cramps like you'd been doing every month since you were twelve."

"Why didn't you say anything?"

"It was your news to tell, Benny. Why didn't you?"

Benny slumped in her seat. "I broke it off with Dan because I was falling for him, Ma. It felt like such a betrayal. To Henny, I mean. I promised him forever. And Dan was one of his best friends, of all people."

"Oh, honey. He was your best friend, too. You both loved Henny so much, but he's gone, and there isn't anything wrong with you two finding happiness together."

"I know that. Now. But I think I might have messed up really bad."

"What do you mean?"

"I never told Dan about the baby," Benny confessed. "I was going to, last night, but he found out before I got the chance and freaked out.

Chapter 22

The Spirit That For Ever Talks

Clarice drove the rest of the way home while Benny spilled her guts. She told her mother everything from falling in love to pushing him away. From realizing she was pregnant to Peter finding the ultrasound picture in his car. From making the decision to let Dan back into her life to completely messing it up by waiting too long. Through it all, Clarice only expressed her surprise that Peter had known but never said anything. As they pulled into the driveway, Benny finally asked, "So what do you think?"

"About what, honey?"

"About Dan, Ma. What have we been talking about for the last half hour?"

"I'm kidding, Benny. You know the answer. He loves you, and will love the baby. Everything is going to be fine, and that's not just a mother consoling her child. I truly believe it, and have all along."

"Do you think I should go see him? Or wait for him to come to me?"

"Well"—Clarice put the car in park—"you owe him an apology. And I suspect he's already been here today, looking for you. I say you go find him."

"What makes you think he was here?"

She leaned over the dash, drawing Benny do to the same, and pointed awkwardly up at Benny's apartment, to the bit of paper fluttering in the evening breeze. "Something tells me that's a note from Daniel."

Benny was out of the car, taking the stairs two at a time before her mother even opened her door. The ligaments in her groin protested. She slowed down, but ripped the note from the door with the enthusiasm of a child at the candy counter.

Tried your cell. I was looking for you. Sorry about last night. Call me. Dan

No teasing. No joke. But he'd been looking for her, so that was something. Benny pulled out her cell phone. Two missed calls from Dan. How had she not heard it ring? Finger poised to return the call, Benny changed her mind and put it away again.

She wouldn't call him. She needed to see him, to see his face when he said what he had to say. Note tucked into her pocket, she ducked into her apartment, grabbed her helmet and hurried—carefully—back down the stairs.

"I'm going out," she called in to her mother, but didn't wait for a response. Clarice Grady would know where she went, and she'd be very happy about it.

Benny tossed her backpack into the makeshift carrier alongside her gardening tools, and kicked-started her scooter. Only after she hit the first bump in the road did she wish she'd taken a moment to use the bathroom. Cricket was starting to take up more interior space. For the first time since seeing the line appear on the pee-stick, Benny happily imagined herself round as a harvest pumpkin, waddling to the bathroom every ten minutes because her bladder was the size of a grape. The image made her smile, and then it made her laugh. Back was her certainty Dan was going to be happy about this. Maybe he was angry she'd waited so long, but he'd get over it. He loved her. She was certain about that too.

Happiness, pure and untainted, started in Benny's toes and bubbled up inside her like soda in a glass. The sensation was as familiar as it was alien, once a part of her every day and forgotten. Still too near the apathy marking the last six years of her life, Benny remembered it with a clarity she didn't have when entrenched in it.

He rode out of this life and onto another road that goes on and on and on. He wants to see where it leads, if it's okay with you.

"I won't go back there, Henny," she said aloud. "I swear I won't. For both our sakes."

Instead of driving through town and out to Division Street, Benny continued south to the cemetery. Dan had been waiting all day, but Henny had been waiting six years. For this last time, he came first.

Old habits died hard, but they did die. Benny parked on the road just below Henny's grave rather than beneath the familiar shade tree. She grabbed her trowel, and headed up the hill to that place for her husband's bones. Tears rolled down her cheeks, but Benny wasn't sad. Not really. Kneeling on the ground outside of the gravesite flower garden she'd maintained for years, she wiped the tears from her eyes. She dug up his grave garden, flower by flower. She gave the marigolds to Frank and

Louise Dillard, gone since 1946 and 1951. The snapdragons went to little Sally Feldman, all alone in her grave since 1973. Pansies and salvia and petunias, Benny spread them around.

The morning glory seedlings wouldn't survive a transfer, and she didn't have the heart to kill them, all things considered. She left them to grow through the summer and to die a natural death at first frost.

As she bent to the forget-me-nots, an engine revved on the street beyond the cemetery, lifting Benny's head. A motorcycle whizzed by, one she had seen around town. Signs and signals made tangible in the living world—she had once been a big believer, and then lost all such faith. At the moment, Benny was content to keep her mind open in both directions, and in any other direction that presented itself.

She turned back to the forget-me-nots, digging them up carefully, taking a bit more dirt than she had with the others. She found an old plastic grocery bag containing the remnants of a lunch long-ago enjoyed in the bottom of her backpack, and placed two of the three plants into it. The third she took to Harriet Farcus.

"You already have a garden," she said, "but I wanted you to have these, too. I'm not sure how any of this works, but I have a feeling there is no single way, no single afterlife, but a whole bunch that sort of overlap. Or maybe I'm just a little nuts-o. That's okay too. Anyway, it's time I let Henny go. There's a road he wants to travel, and I am—was—holding him back. I hope digging up the garden freed him in a way words couldn't, like Carmen said. You'd like her. She was pretty amazing. Anyway, it just seemed right. And it seems right for you to have these."

Benny moved some of the petunia near Harriet's stone and replaced it with the forget-me-nots. Sitting back on her heels, she patted the soil down. On her wrist, the forget-me-nots inked into her skin tickled just enough for her to notice. She wiped the dirt from her arm, traced the tattooed mural, her homage to Henny, and this time she smiled with the memories instead of wept.

Grief was so hard to let go of. She couldn't count the years since his death as wasted. It brought her to this, to Dan, to their baby. It brought her Augie and Harriet. As her mother said, Benny was waking up from too long a sleep, but she was awake now. Wide awake. And that was the important part.

"I won't be cemetery gardening much anymore. But these should grow back. They aren't perennials, but they do re-seed. I'll let Charlie know not to let the landscapers mow them down." Rising to her feet, Benny brushed the dirt from her hands. She tucked the trowel in her back pocket, and picked up the plastic bag holding the other two plants.

"I won't forget Henny. And I won't forget you, Harriet. It's a sworn promise."

Benny placed the last two forget-me-nots into the carrier of her scooter. She drove slowly to the place she and Dan had watched the fireworks—and made some—the night before. Digging a hole near Miranda Greene's tombstone, she smiled a little self-consciously. She planted the flowers.

"My mother misses you," she said. "And sorry about last night. I meant no disrespect, but your son, well…whatever Dan said about this just being a place for bones, I have it on good authority it's a bit more complicated than that. I hope we didn't gross you out."

Benny chuckled softly, her body aching with memory and quickly quelled. For now. Maybe later.

"I don't know what's going to happen with Dan and me, but I want you to know I love him. Gads, I really, really do love him. Crazy, huh?"

Back on her scooter, Benny had one last stop to make. No sorrow attached itself to this one, only joy so tangible she felt like soda in a glass again. She dug Flora's cigar box of soil out of her backpack and brought it along with the last plant to Augie's grave. Wending her way among the tombstones, Benny found a rock slab on the ground where there hadn't been one before. Not a rock slab. A concrete one, embedded with tiny handprints.

Falling to her knees, only just saving the flowers and cigar box from toppling, she touched the slab of concrete once part of Augie's patio. Little handprints, and the initials PF, VF and AF scratched beneath. Had Dan done this before leaving the note on her door? After? It didn't matter. He had done it, not for Augie, but for her.

She sunk the forget-me-nots into the ground between the headstone and the concrete slab. Sitting back on her heels, Benny lifted the cigar box in her hand, flicked open the brass catch, and poured the contents into the hole. Soil from a small village in Campania, Italy mingled with the soil from Flora's garden in Brooklyn, into the good earth of Bitterly, Connecticut. It covered the exposed roots of the flowers, closing the circle left open too long.

"She knew you, Augie," Benny said. "Flora knew who you were all along, and she loved you. There is no forgiveness to be had, because there was never any necessary.

"Love doesn't have to be shouted," she quoted. "Sometimes, love can just be. You loved Flora and she loved you, no matter the circumstances.

Let go, Augie. Let go and see where the road goes next. Maybe she's waiting for you, with Katherine. Maybe they've both been waiting for you all along."

A slight buzzing in her ears became a sensation that began in her midsection and spread. Up to her shoulders, her cheeks, the roots of her hair. And down through her legs, calves, toes. Not the soda-in-a-glass sensation, but warm and fluid, like maple syrup on pancakes. It seeped into her blood, her bones, her beating heart. It surrounded Cricket, soothing her incessant wriggling. Benny wrapped her arms around herself, rocking side to side. Love. That was all it could be. Like her earlier and lingering happiness, it was pure and untainted by life or death, by sorrow or fear. It bridged the intangible, made it real. And when Benny closed her eyes, that flash of Augie she'd accidentally seen superimposed itself over the image from Carmen's album and for an instant, held. Benny kept her eyes closed tight, drew the instant out as long as possible.

"Got it, Augie," she whispered. "I'll never forget you, either. Now go, while you can."

The image faded from behind her eyes. The maple-syrup warmth absorbed completely, but didn't vanish. It would never vanish completely. Cricket, kept still for too long, gave a good kick Benny felt on the outside as well as in. She gasped, and then she laughed softly, cradling her belly and the baby inside.

"Do that when we go see your daddy," Benny crooned, "and he'll be the happiest man on earth."

Benny rose to her feet, brushed herself off, and tamped the soil around the forget-me-nots on Augie's grave. Tomorrow, she'd get her mother started on finding Augie's children, or grandchildren if that was all who remained. Tonight, right this moment, she was going to see Dan and tell him she'd been a fool, she loved him, and they were having a baby—all of which he already knew, but she'd tell him anyway. Benny picked a stem of forget-me-nots from Augie's bunch. She tucked it into the buttonhole of her shirt, got back on her scooter, and left the cemetery just as evening twinkled into night.

* * * *

"That's it then, eh? Another one gone. Good riddance, I say. Bah! That's a lie. I'll miss the fool. He was good company. There used to be so many more. Now there's just me, here inside the gates. I can see others out there, in town. I can feel others nearby. I wonder what it's like, remembering enough to step out. I don't even remember why I don't try, only that I'm a'feared too.

"*I'll miss the girl, too. Benedetta. I'll miss her jabbering. She'll come back now and then, bring the little one to see me, but it won't be the same. She knows too much now. If anyone understands knowledge isn't always a good thing, it's me.*

"*Oh, too close. Entirely too close to remembering. Augie wearied me, made me want things I shouldn't. It's time to get my senses back. It's time to get some rest.*

"*Maybe a year.*

"*Maybe ten.*

"*Maybe just until Benedetta comes back with her wee one.*"

Chapter 23

Only They Who Walk With Dreams

Daniel Greene washed his shovel. Again. He checked his cell. Again. The shovel was as clean as new and there were no missed calls or texts from Benny. She hadn't been at Savvy's, or at home. Neither was Clarice, so that was something. He imagined Benny so angry or upset her mother took her out of town for the day, to get away from him. He wouldn't consider he'd blown it completely, even if he kicked himself over and over for the way he bolted. Dan didn't even know why. He saw the sonogram picture stuck to the refrigerator door and it was all a blur from there, right up until the moment he sank the slab of concrete into the ground covering August and Katherine Fiore's graves.

The calm, then, had been serene. There in the cemetery, during those ghosting hours when most of Bitterly slept and only crickets sang their songs, Dan had sat on the edge of the tombstone and laughed. Softly, at first, then great lungsful of joy that might have sounded mad, coming from the cemetery after midnight. He almost went back to Benny's, but it was late and all they had to say to one another would wait until morning. Dan was exhausted, both mentally and physically. Instead of going home, where Paul and Evelyn were, he parked his truck behind the old cottage currently serving as the cemetery office, found the key under the frog sculpture where Charlie had been hiding it since it was a secret they all kept from his parents, and let himself in. He fell face-first onto the cot in the back room, and was asleep before the dust settled.

It was late when he woke, after eleven in the morning, and he only did so because Charlie kicked one of the cot legs out from under him.

"You're an idiot," Charlie said when Dan told him why he was there. "Get over there now and ask her to marry you."

And that's what Dan did, but she wasn't home. Neither was Clarice or Peadar, but Peter pulled up as Dan was coming down from the second floor, having left a note there for Benny.

"Any idea where your sister is?"

"I'm just getting back from Cape May, so no."

"Oh, right. How was it?"

"Great. It would have been better without Charlotte's new boyfriend. Asshole."

"Tough break, Pete."

Peter shrugged and Dan left, and now it was after eight o'clock and Benny had still not returned his call or responded to his note. The certainty he'd earlier felt was beginning to flag.

"Hey, didn't you hear me calling you?" Evelyn's voice startled the rag from Dan's hand.

He bent to pick it up.

"Apparently not." She moved closer. "You okay? You angry with me?"

Dan hung the wet rag on a peg to dry. He put the shovel back in its place. Finally, he looked at his sister. "No. I'm happy for you. I just hope you know what you're doing."

"I'm completely clueless," she said. "But I'm happy. This feels right. I have to try, you know? We have kids, and we still love one another."

"He seems different. Paul."

Evelyn smiled a dreamy smile. "This is who he's always been behind the costume he wore for his parents and the business world. He reminds me a lot of Henny, actually."

Dan scrunched up his nose. "I thought he reminded you of me."

"Both of you. More surfer-dude than wildman-biker, but easy-going at the core."

"I'll take your word for it. If this is what you want, you know it's what I want for you."

"What will you do?"

"About?"

"You going to keep the house? Stay here in Bitterly."

"To the bitter end." Dan grinned. "I'd like to keep the house. We'll come to some kind of buy-out arrangement. But…"

"But?"

Dan took a deep breath, let it go. The joy wiggling in his gut made it quiver. "I'm going to be a father, Ev."

She paled.

"What? Who?"

He rolled his eyes.

"Okay, dumb question. Details, fella, and I mean now."

He told her everything from that blissful week in February to his amnesiatic freak-out after finding the ultrasound picture on Benny's fridge, except for making love to Benny in the cemetery instead of actually watching the fireworks. There were some things he would keep to himself.

Evelyn listened without saying a word until his story was finished. "It's like a movie. On the Hallmark channel. Give it a Christmas theme and you can sell it for the holiday season."

"Thanks. Your compassion really touches me."

"It's a lot to take in." Evelyn bit her lip. "You watched the fireworks with Mom every year?"

Dan shrugged. "It's just something I do."

"I'd like to think I'd have gone with you, if I knew."

"But you wouldn't have." He smiled. "It's okay. We deal with it differently, is all."

"Did you ever think...?"

"Think what?"

"Never mind. It's dumb."

"Tell me. Come on."

Again she chewed her lip. "I've always kind of wondered if she did it on purpose. Crashed the car, I mean. It was Dad's side of the car that took the brunt."

"Maybe she did it on purpose," Dan said. "Could be, or maybe he'd already started smacking her and she lost control of the car. We're never going to have any real answers, Ev. Let it go."

"But you've thought it."

"Sure."

"Then you haven't let it go, either."

"Yes, I have. I can think a thought without it eating me up. Like right now, I'm thinking how great it would be to tickle you till you pee. But I won't."

"Well, thanks for that."

They laughed softly together, old demons once again quelled in the old, familiar way. Evelyn took his hand and tugged him toward the garage door.

"I saved dinner for you. Come in and eat."

"What did you make?"

"Fried catfish and corn on the cob."

"Sounds like I'm hungry." And he was. Dan was starving. Had he eaten all day? He had no idea.

Outside, the distinct whine of a four-stroke engine got louder, closer. His heart flipped and his belly tumbled. Then tires on gravel. The tinny engine struggling. A headlight coming up the driveway.

"Looks like your baby-mama is here to see you."

"Looks like it."

"You love her?"

"More than I ever imagined possible."

Evelyn kissed his cheek.

"You're going to be an amazing father, Danny."

He might have nodded, or said words of thanks. The blur he'd flown through descended again, but this was not the prior night's mad dash. It was slow. Torturously slow. Yet Dan found himself standing at the top of the driveway, completely incapable of doing anything else.

His mouth went dry.

His heart hammered.

In his mind's eye, he pulled Benny from her scooter, into his arms, and kissed her until any doubt she might still have vanished.

* * * *

Her scooter didn't want to make the climb. It was never good on gravel, and not great on a steep incline. Benny gave up about halfway to the house. She killed the engine, pulled off her helmet. Dan stood at the top of the driveway, still as one of his Casablanca lilies on a windy day.

Benny's heart flipped, a glorious feeling she remembered so well. Henny made her heart flip. She remembered now, without grief. Peter had been right. Love didn't vanish. It made room for more and more if allowed.

She walked the rest of the way up the driveway, only slightly nervous that Dan didn't meet her halfway. His terrified expression said it all. Benny would not balk. She would not let even a smidgeon of doubt rob her of the words she'd been practicing the whole ride over. She plucked the wilting forget-me-not from her buttonhole, and held it out for him. "Well, Daniel Greene, now you know you knocked me up. You going to marry me, or do I get my dad here with a shotgun?"

"He a good shot?"

"Very. I wouldn't chance it."

"Then I guess I have no choice." Dan took the flower from her fingers, then her hand in his. He pulled her to him and kissed her softly.

Benny wrapped her arms around him, kissed him breathless. "I'm sorry it took so long to tell you," she gasped. "I've been a mess."

"I know."

"I felt like I was betraying Henny, falling in love with you."

"Me too, but…"

Benny leaned back just enough. "But?"

"I was okay with it, Benny. We aren't betraying him, even if that's what it felt like. I can't live in the past. Some of it is great and some of it sucks, but there's no changing it. You were Henny's wife. He was my best friend. It was great while it lasted. Now you're going to be my wife, we're going to have a baby, and I'm going to love you both without thinking about him."

Before watching fireworks from his mother's grave, Benny might have believed his words' bravado. Now, in this new moonlight looking up at the man she loved, she understood his courage, his determination to live the best life possible, no matter what the demons of his past had to say about it. She wanted that too, for herself and for her child. Their child. Changes were coming, and not just in her figure or marital status. It was time, long past time, they did.

"Let's go to Bermuda and get married," she said. "Tonight. Okay, it's too late tonight. But tomorrow. And let's not tell anyone until we've left. What do you say?"

"I say I hope you have a passport."

"Damn. How about North Carolina, then? To see Tim. I kind of promised him a visit. He'd be really surprised and happy to see you."

"Okay."

"Really?"

"I don't care where I marry you, Benny, as long as I do. I have a reputation to think of, you know."

"I'll make an honest man of you, I promise." She nudged him. "And when we come home, I don't want to live in my parents' house anymore. Not because it's where I lived with Henny, but because it's time I left home."

"That works out well, because my sister is moving out and I'm buying the house. You…you do want to stay in Bitterly, don't you?"

Benny held him closer, grinned sweetly up at him. "And if I don't?"

"Then I'll have to convince you, somehow." Dan kissed her grin away.

"Not convinced yet," she teased. "Try again."

Dan lifted her into his arms, started for the house.

Benny squealed and wrapped her arms around his neck, kissing him with every bounce. Cricket kicked then, good and hard.

Dan stopped dead in his tracks. "Was that…?"

"It was."

Dan set her onto her feet, kneeled in the grass. He placed his hands where the baby had kicked, and Cricket obliged him with another. Kneeling there, his hands still spread across the just-visible mound of their child, he pressed his lips to Benny's skin.

"Boy or girl?" he asked without looking up.

"A little girl. I've been calling her Cricket, because she jumps around so much."

Dan rested his cheek to Benny's belly, waiting. The baby squirmed but she didn't kick. His hands twitched. He kissed her again, and rose to his feet.

"Cricket, huh? Got anything else in mind?"

She hadn't. Not until this moment. "Irene," she said. "For our mothers. What do you think?"

His eyes might have welled, or it might have been the moonlight on his pale and eerie eyes. "Irene Greene," he said. "It rhymes."

"I like that sort of thing."

Dan nodded and offered his hand. Benny took it and squeezed. Together they went inside to begin forging a new life on the foundation of the old, despite the sorrows, because of the joys. In Bitterly, where they both were born. In the house that Augie built.

Meet the Author

Terri-Lynne DeFino lives in a log cabin in Connecticut, but she's a Jersey girl at heart. Writer, mother, cat wrangler, and self-proclaimed sparkle queen, Terri began writing when she was seven. Though that first story remains locked away in her parents' attic, some of her works include Finder, A Time Never Lived, and Beyond the Gate. Visit her blog at: Modestyisforsuckers.com, or contact her at: terrilynnedefino@aol.com.

Read on for a snippet of Book 3 in Terri-Lynne DeFino's Bitterly Suite

WAKING SAVANNAH

Some memories are best left behind; some refuse to be.

Determined not to let the past define her, Savannah Callowell left all that happened and all she'd been in Georgia for an old farm in Bitterly, Connecticut. Savannah finds peace, friends, and a new life, but she keeps her secrets to herself, and her friends at a distance. But when her foreman retires and offers his son as a replacement, Savannah gets more than she bargained for. Adelmo Gallegos is not the college kid she was expecting, but a grown man running from his own past.

A Lyrical Shine romance coming October, 2016

Learn more about Terri-Lynne at
http://www.kensingtonbooks.com/author.aspx/31624

Chapter 1

Memories of other days

I didn't like fireworks when I was a squirt. That boom. Ugh. It made my stomach swish. Having to sit through them ruined the Independence Day picnics for me. I always wished Mom and Pop would let me go home instead of making me stay. Though, really, our house was too close to town for it to have made a difference.

I can't count the Independence Days that've come and gone since then. Time doesn't pass the same way it used to. One minute it's high summer and the fireworks are booming, the next I'm leaving pebbles in a shoe by the light of the full Hunter Moon. Maybe that's why I'm still here in this Nowheresville of Nowheresvilles having conversations with myself as if someone's listening. As if I'm telling a story.

* * * *

Thunder rumbled in the blue, July sky. Savannah Callowell understood New England storms well enough to know when the mountains would guide the black clouds beyond Bitterly, and when they'd let them in. Today felt like a welcome mat set out for the electric boom.

She stepped into the yard, shielding her eyes from the sunshine. The Fourth of July town picnic had, once again, been a raging success. In all the years since she moved up from Georgia, there had not been a single rainout. The produce was gone down to the last potato. The few soaps and jellies left were mostly back on the shelves in the farmstand store. Lambs in their pens, chickens in their coop, Savvy's was as restored as it could be until the next harvest came in.

"Good morning, boss."

She turned to Benny picking her way across the yard, her eight-month old daughter in a baby-sling strapped to her chest. Savannah waved and smiled and tried to ease the sudden pounding in her chest. Ever since her own life had gone from miserable apathy to marital bliss, Benedetta

Grady-Hendricks-Greene had been on a mission to rid the world of unhappiness. Darling Benny. She had no clue, and Savannah wanted to keep it that way.

"Did you get a good rest yesterday?" Benny asked, hefting her baby higher and adjusting the sling.

"I did, thanks." Savannah rubbed at her forehead. July 5th's typical banger of a headache had dulled back to the familiar throb. "Has Dan recovered from the tug-o-war?"

Benny shook her head, rolling her eyes. "My husband seems to think he's still twenty. He'll survive. Probably just a pulled muscle in his shoulder."

"So, what brings you here this morning? You have the next two weeks off."

"I was hoping you had some of that liniment Darla and Sandra make. Dan isn't just delusional, he's stubborn. He won't go to the doctor about his shoulder even though he groaned all night long."

Savannah laughed. "I think there might be some. Come on in."

They went into the farmstand store. Savannah flipped on the lights. Rummaging around in the lone box as yet unpacked, she called, "Why don't you make us a cup of tea?"

Savannah continued pretending to look for the liniment that had been sitting on top until she heard Benny clattering around in the office. This time of year left her feeling fragile, and unable to cope with the cheerful chattering her friend was famous for, the chattering that usually brought an affectionate smile to Savannah's lips. Watching Benny's transformation the year prior, from grieving widow to wife and mother, had been magical. For a time, Savannah thought, maybe, her joy would rub off. Honor. Determination. The ferocity that took her from temperate Georgia to finicky Connecticut. Such things gave her purpose, but they were not joy.

Tube of liniment in hand, she joined Benny in the air-conditioned office. Her friend was just pouring hot water from the kettle, and Savannah's frazzled nerves became somewhat less so. She handed over the tube in exchange for a steaming mug. Snuggled against Benny's bounteous chest, Irene slumbered as deeply as only a healthy, happy baby could. Savannah remembered the feel of soft, sweet breath on her neck, in her nostrils. She remembered the heft of not one but two contented little bundles on her chest. She remembered.

"Good." She breathed in the peppermint scent. "Is this the chocolate mint?"

"My favorite." Benny wrinkled her nose. "Dan nearly killed me when he found out I planted a patch out back."

Savannah's muscles bunched. Fight? Or flight? She shook it off. "Don't say that. I bet he wasn't even really angry."

"True. But it did take over, and started threatening his precious lilies. I should have known better. Mint is so aggressive."

"Did you sow them directly?"

"What do you mean?"

"Are they in the ground? Or in pots?"

"Ground."

Savannah took another sip. "There's only one way to keep mint from spreading. If you don't want to container-garden, you have to dig up that whole patch and replant a few bunches in those clay chimney flues sunk in the ground. That'll contain the root system. As long as you clip them before they flower and fall, your mint will behave."

"Oh, really? That's so cool. How'd you figure that out?"

"I didn't. Until coming to Connecticut, I never even planted a flower in a pot on my porch. Edgardo and Raul taught me everything I know."

"That's crazy." Benny tugged at a lock of long, dark hair caught in the shoulder strap of the baby sling. Cursing under her breath, she unslung her infant. "I finally got it to grow past my chin and I want to hack it all off again, but I refuse to do the new-mom-pixie cut thing."

Savannah tried not to grimace when Benny set Irene down on the cot in the office. After all the years they'd been friends and co-workers, she still didn't seem to get that there was a reason she gave all her workers two weeks off after Independence Day. Before last year, when Benny came awake again after too many years grieving, her oblivion was understandable. Now, her oblivion felt a little forced. A lot forced. Savannah wouldn't rise to the bait. Not even if Benny asked her outright why she became a hermit for two weeks every July.

"Did Edgardo and Raul get off all right this morning?" Benny sipped, looking at Savannah over the rim of her mug.

"As far as I know. They left on time, at least. I heard them at around three this morning."

"It's so strange to me, them living apart from their families most of the year."

"They must be used to it." Savannah sipped. "They've been working for me for eleven years, and I'm not their first American gig."

Edgardo and Raul Gallegos worked tirelessly from March, when the first seeds were planted in the greenhouse, through to harvesting the last of the pumpkins in the fall. They worked six days a week and took only the two weeks in July Savannah insisted upon to go home to their families in Ecuador.

"We're lucky to have them." Benny leaned in, whispering, "They've got to be getting old though, don't you think?"

"They can't hear you, Benny."

She slouched back in her chair. "You never know who's listening."

"Well, the pictures tacked to the wall in the double-wide never change. Children? Grandchildren? I have no idea. Maybe both."

"Grandchildren? You think? But they don't have a gray hair between them."

"No, but their faces are lined like road-maps. Why do men age so much better than women? Not fair. Not fair at all."

Savannah relaxed despite herself, as the minutes ticked into a chatty hour. Benny laughed easily, drew the same out in her. Even the throbbing in Savannah's head eased. Irene stirred, and then she whimpered. Before she could cry, Benny sat on the edge of the cot and nursed her happy again. The back of her tiny blonde head, thick with curls like her daddy's, made Savannah want to twirl her fingers in the swirl at her crown. Baby hair, like baby breath, was the sweetest of things she could imagine.

Ginger's hair had been dark and sleek. Sally's had been dark and dense. One light-skinned. One darker. And she had loved them so much.

"Sorry," she shook herself out of memory. Benny was no longer sitting on the cot but wrapping her baby into the folds and twists of her sling. "I didn't hear what you just said."

"Your headache okay?"

"My—oh, yes." Savannah touched her head. "It's fine."

"I was just saying that I'd better get this little biscuit to her grandma and grandpa's so I can get ready for my big date. It might take a little while to squeeze myself into the dress I bought. Svelte, I have never been. What was I thinking, buying something so tight?"

"Big date?"

Benny leaned in and kissed Savannah's cheek. "You really are still tired," she said. "It's Dan and my anniversary, remember? You were my maid of honor."

"Oh…oh! Benny, I'm so sorry." Savannah hugged her tight. "Happy Anniversary, sugar. May this be the first of many happy years to come."

"If the rest are only a quarter as happy, I'll count myself lucky. Thanks, Savvy."

Savannah walked Benny outside. It still surprised her to see her friend climb into the hybrid car Dan surprised her with on her birthday, rather than onto the scooter she had always ridden. Strapping the baby into her car-seat, Benny said, "We leave for Bar Harbor tomorrow. You sure you have enough help while I'm gone?"

"Don't start that again." Savannah laughed. "There is almost nothing to do but watch the vegetables grow. Besides, I have enough kids available to fetch and carry for me if I need. Go. Have fun camping. I'm green with envy. Bar Harbor is one of my favorite places on the planet."

"Thanks for the recommendation." Benny tossed the baby wrap into the car and opened her arms to Savannah. "I'll see you in a couple of weeks."

"Bring me back some seashells."

Waving her friend away until her car was a red speck in the sunshine, Savannah's mind raced with all there actually was to do on the farm despite her assurances to the contrary. Watering and staking, feeding, weeding, pest-detecting and eradicating. There were secondary crops to start and seedlings to tend. And the lambs…the spring lambs were nearly ready to go, whether to slaughter or to sale. Picking which ones would go where was a task she hated, and one she wouldn't foist onto someone else, not even the brothers Gallegos, for whom such a task wasn't so heartrending.

Savannah Callowell would dive headlong into all these tasks that were better than being idle this time of year, better than having to be with anyone she loved. The high school students who changed by the year were all she could handle.

Turning to head back to her office, the lists and the planning and the ordering of her present filled her thoughts to capacity. Savannah watched her feet instead of the sky now black and roiling and rumbling thunder, just as she predicted.